SLEEP IN HEAVENLY PEACE INN

Malinda Martin

Other Books by Malinda Martin

Castle Clubhouse Romance Series

The Course of True Love
All's Fair in Love and Fame
The Best Laid Plans
The Write One
Where There's Smoke
Down the Romance Hole

The Midnight Kiss Series

The Midnight Kiss
The Midnight Dance
The Midnight Bride

Christmas in Charity Series

Christmas Grace
Comfort and Joy
Merry Mary
Carol Of The Bells
Faith, Hope, & Mistletoe

Beaumont Family Series

Heartthrob
Heart And Soul
Heart Attack
Heartbreak

The Biggest Part of Me

Tennessee Waltz
Tennessee Shuffle

Christmas Dad

Sleep in Heavenly Peace Inn
Sleep in Heavenly Peace Inn Two
Sleep in Heavenly Peace Inn Three

Forgetting Christmas

LOVE FROM ABOVE
Christian Fiction

The Vow
The Home (Short Story)
The Blessing
The Calling
The City (Short Story)
The Show (Short Story)

Your free books are waiting!

Do you enjoy sweet romance, holiday stories, Christian Fiction?

You can get three stories for free. That's right, three! It's a special gift to you for signing up for Malinda Martin's monthly newsletter.

To get your free books, go to www.malindamartin.com. You'll also receive information on other sweet romance and Christian fiction novels.

Dedicated to the wonderful folks at The Inn at Christmas Place
in Pigeon Forge, Tennessee, a wonderful place to feel the magic of the season.

"Glory to God in the highest, and on earth peace, good will toward men."

Luke 2:14

Chapter One

She saw them coming. The large van swept
down the ruts in the old road kicking up snow in
the cold Vermont air. She was ready for them.
Everything was cleaned and polished. The
Christmas decorations were gleaming. The pantry
and freezers were stocked. Cider was mixed,
wood was chopped, ice skates sharpened, and
snowshoes strung.

The "Sleep in Heavenly Peace Inn" was
ready to receive its guests.

Mary Michaels stopped sweeping the front
porch of the inn to watch the van make its way to
the large farmhouse that would be home to the
guests for the next week. She wondered if Joe had
remembered to fix the leaky faucet in the "It's a
Wonderful Life" bathroom.

Joe. The name of her handyman brought a
quiet sigh to her lips. She had become adept at
hiding her feelings and would continue to do so.

After all, he was the best fix-it man in three counties. She didn't want to lose him. For the good of the inn, that is.

The past three years had been difficult. After her husband had died in Afghanistan, she had looked far and wide to find work that would allow her to make a living and also care for her then two-year old son, Bradley. Eventually she had found the charming inn outside of Stowe, Vermont. The manager seemed willing to take a chance on her as innkeeper, and she and Bradley had happily settled in at the bed and breakfast. The daily grind of taking care of the inn and nurturing her son had helped her work through the grief of loving her husband.

And then Joe Puletti came into their lives. He came to their doorstep, dressed in old jeans and a chambray shirt, a duffel bag over his shoulder. He was tall, over six feet, with jet-black hair that hid dark, brooding eyes. Long, lean, and strong, he looked able to tackle any task given, whether it was conquering the enemy with his bare hands or fixing the kitchen garbage disposal. He looked to be close to forty but it was hard to tell with his constant solemn expression.

Except with Bradley. The man adored the five-year old, playing with him, teaching him, laughing with him. Joe had an infectious, booming laugh that always caused Mary to grin.

When Joe had arrived that day looking for a job, Mary had been unsure about him until he told her that he had been a friend of her late husband Patrick. Mary remembered Patrick writing about a good friend named Joe. After his references checked out, Mary gladly recommended him for the position of handyman for the inn.

That was a year ago and Mary had never had any doubts about the wisdom in having Joe there. She did at times have other feelings, however. Unwanted feelings. In the past year it had been hard not to notice the rough-edged man who had such a tender heart for her son. Joe barely spoke ten words a day to Mary but she found herself looking forward to those ten words. Every time she caught herself thinking about him, she gave herself a mental slap and turned her mind elsewhere. She had to. No handsome, virile man would want a woman like Mary. Not if they knew her secrets.

Mary watched as Joe stopped the van and got out. He gave her a polite nod and headed to the back to unload the suitcases. The doors opened and the guests emerged.

First out were two children, bouncing up and down like two kangaroos finally released into the wild. The boy looked to be about ten and the girl, a few years younger. A slender, petite woman stepped out after them. She whispered something in the boy's ear that made him smile and took the little girl's hand. Must be the mother. Behind her was a man dressed in an expensive business suit. He probably would have been handsome if not for the scowl on his face. The boy walked to him and began chattering. The man looked at him with patience, the scowl leaving. As he put his hand on the boy's shoulder, Mary tried to figure out if the man was the boy's father.

Next out was a beautiful woman whose arrogant expression told Mary that the woman knew her attributes. *Oh my. This one may be a problem.* The woman wore tight jeans, designer boots, and a luxurious faux fur jacket. Her makeup was perfect for her heart-shaped face, framed by long, wavy red hair. She gave the kids a look of disdain and headed toward the front porch.

Last to come out of the van was a willowy woman with brown hair. She seemed to be alone as she lifted her purse and huge tote bag over her shoulder. Looking around at her surroundings, a brilliant smile came over her face, lighting her eyes with what appeared to be excitement and appreciation. Mary couldn't wait to meet her.

As Joe lifted luggage out of the cargo hold, his muscles flexing with the effort, Mary tried to temper the slight flutter in her heart. Clearing her throat, she looked back at the approaching group.

"Welcome," Mary said as she put the broom aside. "Welcome to the Sleep in Heavenly Peace Inn. I'm Mary Michaels the innkeeper."

The two kids were first up the front steps, followed by their mother. She stepped forward to shake Mary's hand. "Hello. I'm Celia Davis and these are my children Kevin and Jenna."

After shaking the woman's hand Mary held out her hand to Kevin and then Jenna. "Hello, it's nice to meet you."

The children smiled, clearly at being treated as adults. "Hi. This place's the bomb!" the boy said.

Mary chuckled. "Well, I'm glad you like it, Kevin. Please come it and get warm. If you'll just step up to the registration table, Angela, the inn's manager, will give you your room key." She held the door open as they walked into the quiet lobby.

The man came next and introduced himself. "Hi. Richard Davis. Do you have Internet access?"

Mary cringed inwardly. The man wouldn't give his family two seconds but couldn't wait to find out about their Wi-Fi. Mary smiled politely, "Yes, we do. Free of charge."

"Great." He followed the others into the building.

Miss Tight Jeans came next, her eyes trailing Richard into the inn. Seeing Mary standing there she said, "I'd like to schedule a rubdown for this evening."

Yes, this one was going to be a problem. "I'm sorry, Miss . . ."

"St. Clair. Genevieve St. Clair." The woman stood waiting for an answer.

"Yes, Ms. St. Clair, but as I'm sure you read in our brochure, we use the spa at the Stowe Mountain Lodge. Reservations need to be made twenty-four hours in advance. I'd be happy to schedule that for tomorrow afternoon."

With a huff of impatience, Genevieve said, "Please do." And followed the others into the inn.

Waiting patiently for her turn to say hello to Mary, the last rider approached. Sticking out her hand, she said, "Hello. My name is Lila Benson." And with a beaming smile added, "Your inn is lovely."

Mary liked this woman. Her handshake was firm and her smile was warm. "Thank you, Ms. Benson. I hope you enjoy your stay."

"Oh, please, it's Lila."

Smiling, Mary said, "Lila, then. I'm Mary." Putting her hand on Lila's back, Mary guided her inside saying, "Let me help you get settled."

Already things were not going well at the registration desk. Angela, an older woman in a red suit, tried to calm down the children's father. "Now, then, Mr. Davis, I'm sure this can be worked out." Angela's melodious voice did little to settle down the annoyed man.

"We asked for two rooms. Is that so hard?" Richard complained.

"I'm afraid it is during the Christmas season," Angela returned calmly. "The request we received from you *was* for two rooms. We faxed back the information that we only had one room available and if this was not satisfactory to please get in touch with us. We didn't hear anything back."

Out of the corner of her eye, Mary caught the two children looking at each other. She had seen that look on her own son's face before. Guilt.

"Well, that's just great. We came all the way from New York and for what? To get cheated out of a room."

Angela's stern expression showed she didn't like his attitude at all. "I'm very sorry, Mr. Davis. If you'd like to leave we can check the airlines for you. Get you on the first flight out."

Both kids looked pleadingly at their father. Jenna pulled on his hand. "No, Daddy. You promised. Please let's stay."

Kevin added, "Yeah, Dad. I like this place. Please?"

"The room is a large one. Our 'It's a Wonderful Life' suite. You could take a look and then decide," Angela said.

Richard looked down at the eagerness in his children's faces. He ruffled his son's hair and winked at his daughter. With softness in his voice he said, "Well, I guess it won't hurt to at least look at the room." Then he added, "Two double beds?"

"Queen-sized. And the suite has a beautiful view of the mountains." Angela held out the key. "It's on the second level. The last door on the right. Joe will bring your luggage up to you if you choose to stay."

"Thank you," Celia said sincerely and gave Richard a glare.

Something's not right there, Mary thought.

The "It's a Wonderful Life" Suite was beautiful. The sitting area had a loveseat with two large armchairs flanking it, all in a beautiful floral of red and green. They faced a fireplace, trimmed with marble. On the mantel were models of buildings from the classic movie, surrounded by cotton "snow." Two beds in matching Dresden plate quilts of gold, red, and emerald green stood at the other end of the large room. A dresser donned a crocheted doily on top, with framed pictures of scenes from the movie. The beautiful oak dressing table sat opposite the dresser and included an upholstered chair in front of it.

Celia and the children simultaneously gasped at the beauty of the room. Richard walked over to the beds to feel their firmness. At the window Celia said, "Kids, come look at this view!"

They ran over and Kevin pointed to the distance. "I can see the ski trails! Dad, come look at this. You're going to take me skiing, aren't you?"

"Of course." He stood and went to another window to look out.

"Mom! I can see a barn. Do you think they have any animals here?" Without waiting for an answer, Jenna continued. "And look! There are trails going into the woods. And what's that? It looks like a small pool."

Placing her arm around her daughter, Celia said, "It's a hot tub, honey. And those trails you see? That's for cross country skiing."

"Could we try it, Mom?" Jenna asked as she looked up at her mother.

"Sure. Now why don't you two go help Mr. Puletti with our suitcases? That is, if we're staying," she said glancing at Richard.

Kevin and Jenna turned to their dad and waited, their expressions hopeful and pleading. "We'll give it a try," he said quietly and was rewarded by two rockets bombarding him with hugs and kisses. Chuckling, he said, "Okay, okay. Go see if you can help with the luggage."

The children ran off, full of energy and excitement. As soon as they left the room, a heavy fog of tension rolled in, filling the air.

"Well, this is great, just great. Did you arrange this, Celia? Just to annoy me?"

"You think I want to be in the same room with you for a week? I'd rather have a root canal," Celia hissed.

"They sent us a fax to explain the situation. You had to have seen it." Celia shook her head. "If you didn't then who . . . Oh, no," Richard muttered.

"Afraid so." Celia sighed. "I caught the expressions on Kevin and Jenna's faces. I think this last family vacation is just a plot."

"What? You mean like . . . they're trying to get us back together?"

"I should have noticed. They've been watching an awful lot of that movie 'The Parent Trap' lately. I was just so busy it didn't click."

"Well, we need to have a talk with them. A serious one, right away. Get rid of all their fantasies."

"Do we have to? I mean there's no reason we can't give them this last vacation together. Do we have to spoil it with talk about what happens after the holidays?"

"I just don't want them getting their hopes up, that's all." Richard ran his fingers through his dark blonde hair and paced. "You know I love those kids, Celia. I don't want to hurt them."

"And what you're doing won't hurt them?" she asked sarcastically.

"That's between us. It doesn't have to affect them."

Celia shook her head. "You are such an idiot, Richard. You really think that the children will come through this without scars?"

"Celia. Do *you* honestly think we can live the rest of our lives together?"

To her horror, Celia's eyes began to tear up. In a small voice she said, "We once thought we could."

His voice lowered. "Yeah, well that was a long time ago." He walked to her. "We've changed Cee. You know it, I know it. It just won't work anymore."

The realization hitting her again, Celia nodded and took a deep breath. She honestly didn't want to shed any more tears. She had shed too many already. "Well, they'll have to come to that understanding soon enough. I'll have a talk with them. In the meantime, let's just get through the next week."

But Richard had already tuned her out. He was looking out at the peaks of the mountains and the ski trails that swerved down the sides. "What? Yeah, sounds good."

Celia looked at her husband. He had already moved on with his life and she wasn't a part of it anymore. Her heart died a little more. She doubted that she would have any heart left at all by this time next month.

She shook her head. It was time for her to get on with her life, also.

Lila opened her door balancing her large purse and her heavy tote. When she entered the "Miracle on 34th Street" room, she sighed in delight. The queen-sized sleigh bed was covered in red satin edged in green trim with matching pillows. The mahogany stained fireplace mantel held pictures from the classic movie. A large armchair was next to the fireplace and a floor lamp with a fringed-trimmed lampshade stood next to it. Lila thrilled in thinking of sitting there by a crackling fire reading one of her books. A small dresser nearby held figurines of Santa and his workshop. The wallpaper that covered the room was a neutral cream with tiny Santa sleighs all over it. The room was charming and instantly put Lila into the Christmas spirit. What a great place to come for the holidays.

Lila took out her small notebook and jumped up on the comfy bed. She took the attached pen out and started writing, wanting to record everything about this trip. This was not only a vacation but also a retreat.

Being a second grade teacher in New York City, Lila didn't earn a large paycheck. However, she was indulging in this vacation for a specific reason. Two months ago she'd received an invitation for her ten-year high school reunion, to be held the next summer. That invitation had made her take a hard look at her life. She was almost twenty-eight years old. The thought of going back, seeing old acquaintances, remembering all the hopes and dreams that she had once had caused her to panic. She needed to think. She needed to re-evaluate where she was in her life.

Since her parents were both dead and she had no siblings, there was no reason to go back to her hometown in Iowa for Christmas. The Sleep in Heavenly Peace Inn was going to be her home for the next two weeks. And she was going to enjoy it—skiing, ice-skating, sledding, everything she could find to experience—and in addition, plan out the life she wanted.

No doubt about it, during her stay she'd craft a wonderful plan for the next ten years of her life.

She was going to return to New York a changed woman.

Chapter Two

The sun was already setting at four thirty. Days were short in a Vermont winter. Short and cold, as the temperature was already dropping below the twenties.

Mary was in the kitchen getting dinner ready. The sunny yellow and white décor always brightened her mood, even on the gloomiest of winter days. She stood by the sink, mixing a batter for homemade biscuits and looking out the back window. Her breath caught in her throat when she saw Joe coming out of the barn and heading for the house. "Stop it," she muttered to herself. This silly schoolgirl crush had to end. Otherwise, she'd make a fool of herself and probably lose the best handyman she could ever have.

Coming in the back door, Joe stomped the snow off his boots. In the mudroom, he conscientiously removed the boots along with his heavy coat. Before going into the kitchen, he stuffed his gloves in his coat pocket and hung the coat and his scarf, a bright blue one Mary had crocheted for his birthday, on a wooden peg.

He walked through the kitchen, pausing to say, "The animals are all taken care of for the night. Let me get washed up and I'll be in to help you." And before Mary could comment, he was gone.

Joe had a small room off the kitchen hallway, at the back of the house. It was very simply decorated, containing a bed, a dresser, a chair, and a lamp, along with a small bathroom. It was perfect for him. He didn't need anymore. He started the shower and began undressing, thinking about the way Mary had pulled her auburn hair away from her face. It was cute that way, although Joe liked it down best. He loved being the handyman of the inn. Not only did it give him a chance to work with his hands in doing a variety of different jobs, it provided him the opportunity to fulfill a promise he made to his best friend before he died—a promise that he was bound and determined to keep.

With the biscuits in the oven, Mary checked the broccoli cheese soup warming on the stove and the roast chicken, potatoes, and vegetables in the warmer.

"What can I do to help?" Joe asked, coming into the kitchen and grabbing a fresh apron from the drawer.

Mary couldn't help noticing the clean pair of jeans and the white buttoned-down shirt he'd changed into. He stood tall and lean, and a pleasure to the eyes. His hair was still a little damp from his shower and Mary could smell the gentle scent of the soap he used. Very alluring. She smiled at her silliness.

"Mary?"

"Sorry. Yes, you can slice the chicken. I'll just toss the salad and as soon as the biscuits are ready we can set the food out."

As Joe worked on the chicken he gave his report of the animals to Mary. The inn didn't really need them but the owner had a soft spot for neglected and abused animals. Currently in residence were one cow, two horses, two sheep, three chickens, five dogs, two cats, and a duck. No one knew where the duck had come from but he seemed to like it there.

As she pulled the biscuits out of the oven and placed them in a ceramic bowl, Mary listened and chuckled at his description of the cats chasing the duck. She wiped her hands on a dishtowel and turned from the counter. Looking up, she found Joe's eyes on her. And froze. They gazed at each other deeply for what seemed like minutes but was only a few seconds. Suddenly a dark haired little whirlwind came barreling into the kitchen, breaking the spell.

"When's dinner. I'm hungry!" Oblivious to the tender looks, the child looked at the bowl of hot bread. "Biscuits! Yay! Mama, can I ring the bell, please?"

Flustered, Mary walked to the worktable to pick up bowls of food for the dining room. "Yes, of course, Bradley. Go ahead." She quickly left the room.

Joe stood still looking after her. He had lost his head for a moment, that's all. Her soft laugh and her elegant movements had entranced him.

This had to stop. There must be a way to stop thinking of Mary in these terms, he reasoned. He grabbed a few more dishes of food, thinking over the problem.

Everyone gathered at the large oak table in the dining room. Food was set on a mirrored buffet next to the kitchen door along with plates. The guests were instructed to take a plate and help themselves.

After being reminded that the guests went first, Bradley stood to the side and waited. When he saw Kevin and Jenna coming, his face lit up. Other kids! Confidently, he walked over to them. "Hello. My name's Bradley Michaels."

"Oh, yes," Celia said coming up behind her children. "You're the innkeeper's son, aren't you?"

"Uh-huh," he replied.

"Wow." Kevin said, clearly impressed. "It must be fun living at an inn in Vermont. Do you ski?"

"Oh, sure." Bradley liked the admiration. He wasn't about to tell Kevin that in the time they had lived there, he had only skied down the small hill in the backyard, and that was only after he had begged Joe to show him how.

"You are such a lucky dog," Kevin said.

"I'm Jenna Davis and this is my brother Kevin."

"Do you like biscuits? My mama makes the best biscuits in the whole world," Quickly moving on to another subject he said, "We've got a new puzzle in the parlor. Maybe you can help me with it later."

Celia smiled brightly. With her hands on the kids' shoulders she said, "I think that would be nice. Thank you for the invitation, Bradley."

"Okay," he said. Seeing the line move, he said something he'd heard his mother say. "Get it while it's hot."

Celia and Jenna chuckled, moving forward. Kevin said, "See ya later, Brad."

Bradley could have jumped to the moon at that moment. The older kid had called him by name—and not just by name, but by a nickname. How cool. He ran into the kitchen to tell his mother.

Celia helped the children with their plates and they sat down. The friendly young woman, Lila, she remembered, sat across from her. The beautiful, rude woman sat a few seats down, keeping to herself. Angela, the inn's manager, came fluttering in. She still wore her red suit and low-heeled red pumps. Her light hair was cut short, around her round face, showing off her red Christmas tree ornament earrings.

"Well, I see that everyone's gotten settled and is ready for a good meal." She walked over to the buffet, generously helping herself to the food. "I hope you loaded your plate. Mary is one of the best cooks in Stowe." She sat down at the head of the table next to Genevieve.

"Rude woman" gave her a disdainful look and said, "Do you regularly eat with the guests?"

Celia looked up at that, thinking how bad mannered. Her eyes caught Lila's and gave an eye roll. Lila couldn't quite smother a smile.

"Well, yes I do, dear. You see, I find it beneficial to be available if guests have any questions or needs. Since everyone is here at dinner, it's a good time to visit." Angela looked around the table. "Oh, my, everyone's not here. Mrs. Davis, where is your husband?"

All eyes turned to her. A slight blush rose on her cheeks. "He's finishing up a phone call. He'll be right down."

"Oh, well, that's good." Angela bowed her head to say a silent prayer over her meal and then took a hearty spoonful of soup, savoring its delicious taste. "You all must try this broccoli and cheese soup. It is wonderful. Soup is one of Mary's specialties."

Richard Davis came rushing into the room. Everyone looked up to see his scowling face. Feeling the need to justify himself he said, "Excuse me, everyone. I had to take a business call." He sat next to Jenna and looked down wondering where his plate was.

"That's all right, Mr. Davis. Please. Grab a plate on the buffet and help yourself. There's plenty of food."

Richard gave Celia an expression that said, "Are you kidding?" Quietly, he rose and went to the buffet.

Lila looked at Angela. "I was just wondering. Are there more guests coming?"

"Yes, indeed. Our next guest should be arriving any minute. He had his own transportation to get him here. He seems a rather important fellow. And there are a few others but I'm not sure when they'll arrive."

"I assume that Mr. Puletti will drive us to Mount Mansfield in the morning?" Richard asked.

"Bright and early. You'll want to hit the slopes before the crowds. Joe will make a run back to the ski resort at noon and then again at three-thirty. You can come back either time. Oh, and if you should need to get back at another time for some reason, call the inn and we'll send him over to pick you up."

"That's very accommodating of you," Celia mentioned.

"All part of the service," Angela said.

"Should be, after what we're paying," Richard said under his breath as he sat down.

"I'm sorry, Mr. Davis, I didn't quite catch that."

Looking up he said, "I just said we're paying for that service. Celia sometimes gets overexcited about the least little things."

Incensed, Celia said, "Do not try to explain me away. I can speak up for myself and I happen to think it's very nice that the inn will come pick you up anytime from the slopes."

"I'm just saying that for the amount of money we're paying for the luxury of being in *someone's house*, there had better be some perks. That's all."

"You expect everyone to cater to your needs, Richard," Celia murmured.

"When I'm paying a lot of money to them, yes, I expect it."

"You know, a little gratitude would go a long way. You might even be able to teach your children something." Her voice lowered when she added, "instead of breaking promises because you're working yourself to death."

"At least I'm teaching them about good ol' hard work and how to get ahead in life," Richard's voice rose.

"I guess that depends on your definition of getting ahead in life," Celia said matching her husband's tone.

"All I was trying to do was keep you in baubles, darling."

"Me and who else? And do not call me darling, you know how I hate that!"

"Well, *darling*, maybe other women appreciate all the hard work I do!"

Joe, Mary, and Bradley came running from the kitchen. Kevin was staring at his food, Jenna was picking through hers, tears in her eyes. Everyone else was silent. Celia felt her face turn red.

How did he always do that to her? Get her so riled up that she forgot about her surroundings, especially her two precious children sitting beside her. "I am so sorry, everyone. Our behavior is just . . . well, it's inexcusable. Please forgive us."

Richard chimed in. "I agree, totally. Please don't mind us. You see, we're getting divorced."

"Mr. Davis!" Angela cast an anxious look at Jenna and Kevin, who still had not looked up. "The children."

"It's all right Ms. . . . ah, Ms. Angela. Celia and I are already legally separated. The children know all about the divorce. They're all right with it, aren't you?" he leaned over and squeezed Jenna's shoulders. Jenna kept silent. Richard turned back to Angela. "Our divorce will be final after the holidays."

Suddenly Genevieve, who had been positively bored, was now taking great interest in the conversation. "Really?" she purred.

"Yes," Richard said. "The kids had the idea of us all spending a week together on vacation before that happens. So, that's why we're here. But Celia was right. There was no excuse to air our grievances in public. We'll try to call a truce."

Celia thought she heard Angela murmur, "The poor dears," but she could have been mistaken.

The rest of the dinner Lila and Celia chatted—about children, about Lila's job as teacher, and Celia's part-time job as pediatric nurse. Lila was amazed. Celia was a wonderful woman in her opinion. She was so sorry to think of the pain of going through a divorce that Celia must be feeling.

She looked down at the other end of the table. Richard didn't seem to be in too much pain. He was talking to Genevieve and they both seemed to be enjoying the conversation. It made Lila feel sad.

When dessert of apple crisp with vanilla ice cream was served, Kevin's eyes lit up. "Oh boy! My favorite!"

Mary put a bowl of chocolate syrup with a small ladle in the middle of the table. Jenna looked up and beamed a bright smile. Mary smiled back. "You like chocolate sauce on your vanilla ice cream?"

"Yes. How did you know?"

"I didn't. Angela suggested it." She leaned down to the little girl and said, "I'm guessing Angela knew. I don't know how she knew, but she did. She's quite amazing."

Jenna looked at Angela. Angela was taking a big bite of apple crisp and ice cream covered in chocolate syrup. When she caught Jenna looking at her, she winked at the girl. Jenna's eyes grew very big. But only for a second. Then she got busy on her ice cream with chocolate syrup. The interaction was precious and made Lila smile. Yes, this was a good place.

The front door opened and a deep voice was heard saying, "Hello?"

"Oh, that must be another of our guests. Excuse me, please," Angela said as she hurried to the front lobby. A few minutes later, the man was escorted back to the dining room.

When Lila saw him, she let out a small gasp.

He was tall, about six feet, with wavy dark brown hair and glittering green eyes. Everything about his face was slim, his nose, his lips, his cheekbones. There were lines that deepened from his eyes, indicating a busy, high stress job. He looked up at everyone and his smile revealed dimples on both sides of his cheek, framing a mouth of brilliantly white teeth.

And Lila knew him.

Her hands immediately began to sweat. She worried them together in her lap, suddenly not interested in the delicious dessert. Her mind was quickly working out how she could leave the table without being introduced to the man.

Angela gently took the man by the arm of his expensive sports jacket. "Everyone, I'd like you to meet Mr. Dan Hamilton. He's a world famous travel writer and he'll be staying with us, working on a story about the Sleep in Heavenly Peace Inn. Isn't that exciting?"

Whispers of interest and greeting filled the air as Angela introduced the group to Dan. "Now, why don't you sit down right here next to Lila. I know you're tired from your trip so I'll get you a plate of dinner while you relax."

"Actually, I've already eaten." Then viewing the delicious apple crisp he added, "But I think I will have a little of that dessert." Angela smiled and dished him up a plate of apple crisp with ice cream.

"Hamilton. I think I've read some of your stuff. Didn't you have an article in the Wall Street

Journal on the advantages of traveling in Asia?" Richard asked.

"Yes, I did," Dan said as he poured a bit of chocolate sauce over the ice cream.

"Fascinating. I'm planning my first trip next year," Richard added. Celia and the children looked at their dessert.

"You'll love it," Dan said moaning over his first bite of the scrumptious dessert.

"It's so nice to have you join us for the week, Mr. Hamilton. We love our little inn and I'm sure that you'll love it as well," Angela said.

"If all the food is as good as this dessert, you can bet I will. I've got to be careful I don't put on any weight. What activities do you have around here?"

Angela's face lit up. "We've got cross country skiing right out our back door. The trails are wonderful. For downhill skiing, Mount Mansfield is a short ride. We have plenty of snowshoes if anyone wants to take a walk. And in the back of the property is a small frozen lake that we ice skate on."

Dan had taken a small note pad from his shirt pocket and was writing it all down. "Sounds great. Then I can eat as much of this delicious food as I want."

"Exactly," Angela agreed, chuckling.

Dan made a few more notes and asked, "Funny, I couldn't find the name of the owner in any of my research." He looked up at Angela. "Got a name for me?"

With an angelic smile, she answered, "Not really."

He frowned slightly. "Oh? And why's that?"

"The owner likes to stay anonymous so as not to take any attention away from the inn." Before Dan could ask another question, she smiled and walked to him. "More dessert?" she asked, heaping a large spoonful of apple crisp on his plate.

Everyone got back to their eating and talking among themselves. Lila held her breath. If she could just excuse herself and go back to her room—for the next week. Then Dan turned to her. "Could you pass the water pitcher, please?"

"Surely," Lila mumbled and handed it to him.

"Thanks," he said really looking at her for the first time.

Lila could feel sweat running down the back of her neck. Her heart was beating so fast, it was close to jumping out of her chest as his stare lingered over her face. Lila gave him a slight smile and looked forward, sipping her hot coffee.

Finally, when Lila thought perhaps he'd go back to his dessert and leave her alone, he said the words she had been dreading to hear.

"Do I know you?"

Chapter Three

There are times in everyone's life when they wish they could be anywhere else doing anything else except where they were and what they were doing. For Lila, this was one. She searched her brain to come up with a sophisticated and coherent answer to the simple question. When nothing came she simply said, "I'm Lila Benson."

Confusion filled his face. Obviously He was struggling to place the name and the face. "The name sounds familiar but you're going to have to give me a hint."

Wasn't that just the way it always was? Some people could take the superior position of, "I know you passed through my life at some point but I just don't remember you." As if to say, "You really weren't important enough for me to remember." And other people are the ones that don't forget anyone in their entire life—especially anyone who made a fool of them.

Knowing that she wasn't going to get out of this, Lila said, "Iowa. Bennett Crossings High

School." She waited for the laughter to start. The blush had already begun to creep up her neck.

A moment later, Dan's face brightened. "Lila. Of course, Lila Benson. One of the smartest people in our graduating class. Well, I'll be. Come over here and give me a hug." Dan pulled Lila over and hugged her warmly.

Her head was spinning. Didn't Dan remember high school? Didn't he remember that he was the popular guy and she was the nerd? Those rules don't change even out of high school. Do they?

"So, tell me all about yourself. What have you been doing since high school?"

Lila couldn't help it. She was thrilled. Even though it had been ten years since school, she was talking to the starting quarterback of their football team. She told him about going to New York University and deciding to stay in The Big Apple to teach.

Dan listened with interest. "Have you kept in touch with anyone from high school?"

"Only a few. I doubt that you know them. We really didn't travel in the same circles then."

"Maybe not. But I do know that I would have flunked classical literature if it hadn't been for you. You know, I can still quote part of Romeo and Juliet? It's come in real handy over the years, if you know what I mean." Dan flashed his smile at Lila.

She plastered on a smile to return. "I'm sure it has. Well, if you'll excuse me, I think I'll retire for the evening."

"Lila, you can't go. Angela told me there'd be hot apple cider in the parlor." Dan leaned down to whisper in her ear. "And at ten o'clock they open the bar in the lounge for the real drinks. Meet me there, let me buy you a drink for old time's sake."

She was tempted. After all, they weren't teenagers any longer and she wasn't a naïve little girl who was hopelessly in love with him. She was an adult who had matured from silly schoolgirl crushes.

Had he outgrown the ways of the selfish teenage male? Surely he wouldn't embarrass her like before. "Okay," she said and excused herself, thanking Mary for the wonderful meal.

Lila walked back to her room to freshen up. She put on more lipstick and dabbed a little perfume behind her ears. Looking in the mirror, she studied herself. Her light brown hair was pulled away from her face in a chignon against the back of her neck. Her eyes were an indefinable color which people tended to label hazel. Her gray, wool slacks were loose as was her black sweater. She wore a small strand of imitation pearls that her parents had given her one Christmas. Her reflection told her she was not so far removed from the shy, plain senior that Dan would have remembered.

She sighed heavily, wondering what it would be like to be more . . . more . . . well, like Genevieve, without the attitude. Lila yearned to be more confident and beautiful. She should have been working on herself all these years but she'd been too busy. She was always too busy.

Lila took out her notebook and began writing goals for herself. Somehow she would work on her looks. She would work on her self-confidence. She would learn to really like herself. Then looking back in the mirror she decided to start tonight. She took down her hair and brushed it until it gleamed. The light caught the glow of it, making her eyes sparkle with pride. If anything, she did have good hair.

Seeing her sweater and pearls, she decided to change into a turquoise turtleneck that clung to her upper body. A necklace of sparkling silver gems was added and she returned to the mirror. Not a bad start, she thought as she left her room, hopeful for the first time in a long time.

The glow from the massive fireplace in the parlor made the room golden and warm. Everyone had gathered after dinner for cider, conversation, and games. Two sofas faced each other in front of the fireplace, another one sat in the bay window that looked out on the front yard. Dan and Genevieve sat at the bay window sofa quietly talking. Angela sat by the fire, knitting. Across from her on the other sofa was Celia, reading. There was a large urn of hot apple cider along with Styrofoam cups on a small table next to the fireplace. Bookcases flanked the sides of the fireplace, filled with classic hardbacks ready to be revisited.

A round table with a large puzzle on it was tucked in a corner and on the opposite side of the room was a rectangular table with benches on each side. It was there that Bradley was working on his puzzle.

He didn't look up as Jenna and Kevin came into the room but kept his head low, intent on his puzzle. The two kids saw him and after a nod from their mother, they headed over to him.

"Hi Brad," Kevin said.

Even the greeting from the older boy didn't cheer Bradley. "Hello," he mumbled.

Jenna and Kevin looked at each other, and sat on one of the benches. "What's the matter, Bradley?"

Bradley wiped his eyes with the back of his hands. "My mama yelled at me."

Thinking to himself that that wasn't so bad, Kevin said, "Bummer. How's the puzzle going?"

"Okay. I can work on it for an hour and then I have to go to my room."

"What happened, Bradley?" Jenna asked.

With big, watery eyes he looked up at the two children and told them the story. After dessert, he, Mary, and Joe were in the kitchen. They were cleaning up, talking and having a good time being together. Bradley decided to put his plan into action.

He could never remember having a dad, and he wanted one. Badly. So, he had decided that Joe would fit the bill—he was nice, he played with Bradley, and he could fix anything, a big plus in Bradley's book. The trouble was that his mom and

Joe never seemed to spend any time together when they weren't working. So Bradley had the idea that after dinner, they should go for a walk together. He had seen it in a movie, where the man and woman went for a walk at night and they got all mushy and started kissing. That's what he had planned for his mother and Joe.

"Bradley, I can't go for a walk," Mary had said. "I have linens in the dryer that I have to see to. Maybe Joe can take you."

"Yeah, how about it, sport? We can check on the animals one more time before turning in."

This wasn't working out the way Bradley had intended. "No. You and mama need to go. If you don't how will you start kissing and stuff?"

Mary dropped the pan she was drying, her cheeks turning red. She was furious. Joe couldn't help but to grin.

"Bradley Alistair Michaels! What's gotten into you?"

"Well, how is Joe going to be my dad if you don't get married and how are you going to get married if you don't kiss and how are you going to kiss if you don't go for a walk together at night?" Then cupping his mouth in his hand for a stage whisper he turned to Joe and said, "I saw it in a movie." Joe had the audacity to chuckle.

"Bradley! Go to your room this instant! When I'm finished here, we're going to have a very long talk!" she shouted.

Bradley wasn't used to being yelled at by his mom. His lower lip began to tremble. "But I promised Kevin and Jenna that I'd see them in the parlor. We were going to work on my puzzle."

She blew out a breath. "All right. We don't want to disappoint the guests. You may go to the parlor for one hour and then go to your room. I can't believe you would think that Joe and I . . . that we . . . and you . . ." Another heavy sigh. "Excuse us." She grabbed Bradley's arm and pulled him into the mudroom. "Bradley, that was a very bad thing you just did. You embarrassed Joe and you put me in a very uncomfortable situation. You—"

"What's 'barrassed? Is it funny, because Joe was laughing," Bradley said.

Mary's face tightened. "Never mind. You are never and I mean never to try to get Joe and me together. We're just friends and we'll never be anything more. I'm sorry you don't have a father. Believe me, I'd do anything if I could change that but I can't. Now, go work on your puzzle with our guests before I really let you have it." She grabbed her coat, put it on over her apron, and went out the back door into the night. Bradley scrunched his brows, completely confused.

He shuffled back through the kitchen trying not to cry. Joe came to him and gently put his hand on his shoulder. "Hey Bud. You know your mother loves you, right?"

His head down, Bradley said, "Yeah," and kept walking.

"Well, maybe the timing was off," Jenna said to him.

"Huh?"

38

"I heard my mother say that before. Maybe it wasn't a good time for them. I mean they were busy with the dishes, right?"

Bradley sighed dramatically. "Yeah, I guess so."

As they worked on the puzzle and quietly thought about the problem, Richard came into the parlor, ignoring Celia who sat by the fireplace. "Kids, I have a few calls to make. I'll be in the room for a couple of hours," he said looking at his watch. "Then at ten I'm going to come down to the bar for a drink." Looking at them, his hands on their backs he said, "You both okay? Having fun?"

"Sure, Dad," Kevin said. "But why don't you help us with this puzzle for a while?"

"Like to, partner, but I've really got to get to these calls. Maybe tomorrow night."

"You are taking us skiing tomorrow, aren't you?"

"You bet." He casually dropped a kiss on each of their heads and left the room. As the kids watched him go, they saw their mother fold the newspaper she'd been reading and put it down. She stood and putting on a smile went to them.

"I'm going for a little walk, kids. I'll be back soon." Even though she tried to hide the tears in her eyes, Jenna and Kevin saw them. They looked at each other with painful expressions.

Not understanding the misery of the kids, Bradley said, "So, when are you getting . . . what was the word . . . uh, a divorce?"

"Next month," Kevin muttered.

"Oh." There was silence as they worked on the puzzle. "What's a divorce? Is it a toy or a game?"

Jenna and Kevin looked at each other and Kevin tried to explain. "It's where a mom and a dad don't like each other anymore and decide to split. My dad doesn't live with us. We only see him on every other weekend. He calls us every few days." Kevin sighed. "It really sucks."

"Kevin, we're not supposed to use that word," Jenna gently reprimanded.

"Can you think of a better way to describe it?"

Jenna thought. Looking down, she said, "No. It really does suck."

"We thought if we had this vacation together, maybe they would see that they really do love each other and that we belong together. But so far, all they've done is argue. Or ignore each other."

Bradley didn't know what to say. He hated not having a father but he couldn't imagine having a father and watching him leave him and his mom. The kids were quiet as they worked on their puzzle.

Lila entered the parlor, and noticing Dan and Genevieve sitting on the couch talking, walked to the bookshelves. Finding Gone With the Wind, one of her favorites, she sat at the round table and began reading.

She tried to concentrate on the words but could only hear the quiet hums of Dan and Genevieve's conversation. No big deal, she thought. She was a big girl and Dan could talk to whomever he liked. He didn't have to speak to her.

Dan stood from the sofa and approached Lila, her heart pounding at the sight.

"Hey, Lila," Dan said. She looked up into beautiful sea green eyes. "I don't mean to disturb you but could I borrow that chair next to you?" Without waiting for an answer, Dan took the chair over to the bookshelves. He stood on the chair reaching to the top shelf and pulled an old atlas down. Returning the chair he smiled at Lila and said, "Thanks." A second later he was sitting next to Genevieve, sitting very closely, as they looked through the atlas.

Lila blinked. What had just happened? Nothing, that was what. Lila felt like such a fool. Nothing ever changed. Heaving a sigh, she looked around the room and saw the three children looking glumly down at their puzzle. Well, at least she was good with children. She set her book down and walked over to them.

"Hey, kids. Why the sad faces?"

The children looked at each other. No one spoke.

Lila understood this. After all, she was used to spending her days with children. She knew how reluctant they could be to talk to an adult. She couldn't blame them. Taking a seat on the bench next to Bradley, she said, "I know. No one can trust the adult. But my kids, once they get to know me, tell me anything and everything. I never tell their secrets."

"You have kids?" Bradley asked.

"Sure do. Twenty-six of them."

"Wow!" Bradley exclaimed.

Lila couldn't help chuckling. "I'm a teacher. I teach second grade in New York." When she saw the expressions of Kevin and Jenna, she thought she'd better clarify the situation. "But, I'm on vacation. So, no teaching while I'm here. Only fun."

Kevin and Jenna exchanged a look. Lila started helping with their puzzle while they made up their minds.

Jenna finally said, "We're bummed about our parents. We were hoping this vacation would fix things, not make them worse."

Lila's heart cringed at that. She reached across the table and held Jenna's hand. "Aw honey." She didn't try to appease or correct or advise. She just held Jenna's hand tightly.

"Yeah, and I've just got to have a dad. Time's running out." Lila looked at little Bradley. "Mom says I'll be grown by tomorrow and before that happens I want her and Joe to get married so he'll be my dad."

Lila smiled tenderly at him. "I don't think she meant you'd be an adult by tomorrow. That's just an expression. It means you're growing up quickly."

Bradley thought about that. "But I still want a dad."

"I know you do, sweetheart." What could she say to these precious children? They were all dealing with things that weren't fun. And here it was the most wonderful time of the year—or it was supposed to be.

Looking out the window, Lila starred. "Kids! Do you see what I see?" She pointed to the starry night. They all looked out the window to see a shooting star crossing the sky. "Want to make a wish?"

"What good will that do?" Kevin asked.

"Haven't you ever heard of 'When you wish upon a Star'?" Bradley asked, demonstrating his superior knowledge of animated movies.

"I thought that was Pinocchio," Jenna said. "And the evening star, not shooting stars."

"It works for all people and all stars, doesn't it Miss Lila?"

"Well, maybe since it's Christmas, it might give wishing a double boost. What do you think, Miss Lila?" Jenna asked.

Lila smiled at the three. "It couldn't hurt, could it? Come on. You'd better hurry up and make your wish. The star's almost out of sight."

All four turned to the window and looked out. Each one voiced their own wish in their minds and wished as hard as they could.

At that moment, the front door opened and two men came walking into the house and into the parlor, tracking in a light scattering of snow. All three children looked up and gasped.

Even Lila did a double take as they all stared at the two men.

Chapter Four

"It's Santa Claus," Bradley whispered in reverent respect.

"And that's got to be an elf," giggled Jenna, whispering back.

Kevin looked at Lila. "Miss Lila, do you see what I see?" Kevin had not been too sure about wishing on the shooting star but had thought why not. Seeing the two men in front of him brought a chill down his spine as if something big was going to happen.

Angela jumped up from her seat and walked over to the men. "Well, I was wondering when you two would get here." She hugged each one warmly. "Everyone, I like to introduce two more guests. This is Sam and his assistant Eldon."

The man she indicated was named Sam was the spitting image of Santa Claus. He was medium height with white shiny hair, a white beard, and white moustache. His eyes were a bright blue and twinkled, just like the story said. His belly was not as fat as some would suppose, though it was ample enough. He greeted the group with a, "Good evening," and then laughed. Not a robust, gut-wrenching laugh or a small snicker. It was a deep chuckle that could easily be heard as a "ho, ho, ho." The kids looked at each other, their eyes bulging and their mouths hanging open.

The man next to Sam, called Eldon, was short. Not midget short, but probably about the height of ten-year old Kevin. The man's expression was one of irritation. He stood next to Sam, clearly evaluating their surroundings.

Jenna whispered, "Sam could be a nickname for Santa."

"And Eldon could be code for elf," Bradley whispered back.

Kevin smiled at all this. It was fun to pretend anyway. "I don't know, you guys. The short man looks mad at something. I didn't think elves were mad."

Thinking, Bradley said, "He probably had a long trip coming from the North Pole. He's tired."

After introducing them to the adults, Angela led the two men over to where Lila and the children sat. "This is Miss Lila Benson." Lila nodded in greeting. "And this is Bradley Michaels, Mary's little boy, and Jenna and Kevin Davis. You can meet their parents later."

"Are you Santa Claus?" Bradley just couldn't resist asking.

Sam laughed a little bigger this time. "Some people do make that assumption. But my name's Sam."

Bradley pointed to Eldon. "Is he an elf?"

Sam's laughter continued. "No, little one. He's just short."

"Vertically challenged," Eldon asserted. "Hey kid. Do I look like I have pointy ears or pointy shoes to you?"

"Now, now, Eldon. It's an honest mistake. But for the life of me, with your poor attitude I can't understand how anyone would think of you as one of Santa's elves." Angela laughed with Sam.

"Yeah, yeah, yeah. Listen, could I have our key? The 'Frosty the Snowman Suite' right? Two double beds with electric blankets? I'm always cold."

"Of course, Eldon," Angela said pulling out a key from her skirt pocket.

"Thanks. I'm really tired after the long trip." Bradley looked with superiority at the other children. They grinned. "I'm going up. Sam, you yak all you want to. Just don't wake me when you come in."

Sam slapped Eldon on the back. "I'll be as quiet as a mouse."

"Come on, Eldon," Angela said. "I'll make sure you're all settled in."

After she led Eldon out, Sam said, "Now, what are the four of you doing tonight?"

"We're wishing on a shooting star. The wishes will come true, don't you think?"

Sam chuckled. "Well, I can't say for sure but I know that Christmas is a time for wishing."

"That's what I said. Isn't that what I said?" Jenna asked suddenly finding her voice.

Sam sat down and started helping with the puzzle and Bradley stood and walked to him. With eyes big and shining, he said, "Can I tell you what I want for Christmas?"

"I'm not Santa, Bradley. But . . ." Sam bent and scooped Bradley up onto his lap. "I'd bet my last dollar that what you want most for Christmas is whatever you wished for on that star. Am I right?" His eyes grew big and he nodded.

"It's good to wish but if it's important to you, you need to do more than just wish."

Suddenly interested, Kevin asked, "What do you mean?"

Smiling, Sam simply said, "You have to believe."

Returning the smile Lila said, "That's right. In fact, I'm going to go back to my room now and start believing. Good night, kids. Sam."

"Good for you, Miss Lila," Sam said to her as she left the room.

"I don't know," Kevin said honestly. "This isn't only a wish, it's a miracle."

Sam put Bradley back on his feet and stood. "Anything is possible, Kevin. Life is full of potential with the dawn of each new day." Looking directly into Kevin's eyes he said, "Sometimes things work out and sometimes they don't. But . . ." Sam's eyes burned into his. "A miracle can't come true unless you believe a miracle can happen."

As Sam turned and left the room, he looked back at the three children and putting a finger at the side of his nose, he winked.

"Did you see that? Did you see that! That's Santa Claus or my name's not Bradley Michaels."

Bradley jumped up and down and Kevin didn't know quite what to think.

"Kevin, Sam didn't come until we wished on that star. It's a sign. There's still a chance." Jenna smiled at her skeptical brother.

He sighed. "I hope you're right. This is probably our last chance."

The following morning, breakfast was served at six enabling skiers to get to the chairlifts by the opening time of eight. Soft strains of classical music played in the dining room. The smell of scrambled eggs and bacon, pancakes and hot maple syrup, and fresh ground coffee filled the air, inviting even the soundest of sleepers to rise.

Lila, Dan, and Genevieve sat on one side of the table, all a little bleary-eyed. Sam sat at the head of the table with a big smile on his face, thoroughly enjoying his breakfast. Eldon was next to him, his face buried in his plate, eating for all he was worth.

Jenna and Kevin sat on each side of their father, barely able to conceal their excitement. Richard was enjoying their chatter. And the meal.

Celia came in and sat on the other side of Jenna, moaning with pleasure when she saw the coffee pot on the table. "I could use a gallon of this," she remarked pouring the hot liquid and adding cream and sugar.

Digging into his pile of scrambled eggs, Richard said, "Didn't sleep well?"

"No." She looked over at Jenna. "Someone kicks in bed."

Jenna looked apologetically at her mom. "I'm sorry, Mom. I'll try to be still tonight."

Celia laughed. "I'm sure you will be. In fact, I'm going to make sure that you are so tuckered out after skiing today that you won't move all night long."

"You coming with us, Cee?" Richard asked continuing to give his attention to his meal.

Celia saw the hopeful looks on her children's faces. "Yes, of course. Even though I know my body's going to rebel. Gee, I haven't been skiing since . . . I can't remember the last time."

Richard looked at the ceiling. "It was New Years. About five years ago. Your folks kept the kids and we went to Smuggler's Notch."

"Ah, yes. I remember." As Celia thought about it, her face heated.

Richard looked at her and grinned. He knew what she was thinking because he was thinking the same thing. It had been a wonderful weekend. So wonderful, in fact, they'd thought she'd come home pregnant.

The Inn's van made its way to the Stowe Mountain Resort filled with excited passengers. Bradley sat next to Kevin and listened with adoration as Kevin and his dad looked over the trail map, plotting their runs. After Joe dropped the skiers off at the lifts, he would be taking Mary and Bradley into town. They would do a little shopping while he went to the hardware store to pick up some supplies.

The mountains of the ski resort stood before them, majestic and proud. There had been a good snow overnight and the power would be fresh and fun. The sun was shining now, giving warmth to the frigid weather. It was a perfect day for skiing.

It was half past seven when Joe pulled up to the ski resort. Everyone piled out. Richard paused to help Genevieve down and a look passed between the two. Celia saw it and quickly looked away. Kevin also saw it, his face falling. Sam caught his eyes just then and gave him the "finger by the nose and wink." Kevin managed a small smile for him.

After being dropped off, Dan walked to the lodge. Sam and Eldon, each carrying duffels, walked towards the "Children's Adventure Center." The others walked over to the rental offices to get skis, boots, and poles. Jenna was so excited she kept asking questions. "Why do we need poles?" "Why are the boots so heavy?" "Why are my skis longer than yours?" "Why do I have to wear a helmet?" Richard was happy when they were finally able to make it out of the building without his losing his patience.

They went first to a small hill called the "Bunny Slope." There, Richard and Celia instructed their children in the basic technique of downhill skiing. Satisfied the kids were ready, they all headed for the chairlift. Celia rode with Jenna and Richard rode with Kevin. They got ready to disembark before Richard remembered to instruct Kevin on the way to exit the chairlift. When Kevin stood on his skis, he was a little off balance and went toppling over on Richard, thus blocking the exit. The operator stopped the chairlift.

Kevin was mortified. Richard also, but he tried to encourage his son. They chose a "green" trail to begin with, an easy one and started down, Richard in the front, then Kevin, Jenna, and finally Celia. Richard began enjoying the experience so much that he didn't notice that he turned into a "blue" trail—a more advanced run. Celia had tried to yell to him not to take the turn, but he couldn't hear her. As they faced a rather steep decline, Richard whizzed down it like a pro. The children stopped and stared. Swallowing hard, Kevin started down, very slowly, very cautiously.

"Mom, I can't go down that," Jenna said.

"Just take it slow and easy, like Kevin. Follow his tracks."

Taking a deep breath, Jenna started down. Halfway, her courage gave out on her. She screamed and then sat on her bottom and slid the rest of the way down to where Richard and Kevin were waiting.

Celia came closely behind Jenna and reached down to take the scared and crying girl in her arms. "I tried to warn you. Didn't you see the blue sign? They're not ready for blue trails yet. I yelled at you to stop but did you listen to me? Of course not."

Richard felt terrible. "I didn't hear you." Looking at his daughter he said, "Jenna, sweetheart, Daddy's sorry. I'll stick to the greens from now on, okay?"

Through her tears, Jenna said, "Okay, Daddy."

There was one more steep slope before they got back to a green trail. Richard took some extra time instructing the kids before they all started down. When Jenna made it down without falling, she squealed, "I did it!"

Smiling, Richard said, "You sure did, honey." He looked up at Celia who was apparently still angry with him since she was scowling. *Whatever.*

They came to a crossroads where several trails intersected. As Richard and Celia were arguing about which one to take, Jenna started sliding down one of the paths. Not her choice, but apparently her skis had their own idea. "Mom! Dad!" she called. Kevin rolled his eyes at her.

Richard said, "Well, I guess we're taking that one."

After making it down the trail, the little group took the chairlift back up. This time Richard explained how to get off the chairlift to his son. When they approached the exit, they both got ready. This time, Kevin disembarked smoothly but his pole got tangled with his ski, causing him to veer right, into the chairlift operator, sending them both down into the snow. Again the chairlift was stopped so they could get up and out of the way. Again, Kevin was mortified.

This time down the trail, the kids did better. They were growing in their confidence on skis and enjoying the ride. In the lead, Richard decided to go a little faster, seeing if the kids would try to keep up with him. At the bottom of one of the slopes, he turned to watch his family come down.

"His family." The words seemed to burn in the back of his mind. The "family" would be no more after the holidays. He mentally shook his head and looked for the kids. Kevin was coming down like a hotshot. Hitting an especially big mogul, he went airborne. Richard's whole being was on high alert as he watched him come down and skid to a stop beside him.

Pleased and, yes, shocked, Richard said, "Well done, Kevin. That was some trick."

"Thanks, Dad." Kevin was glad to take the credit. Inside, he was still shaking from his unwanted flight.

As the others joined them, Jenna asked her dad to adjust one of her bootstraps. He dropped his poles and bent to fix it but when he stood he started sliding backwards. Before he could stop himself, Richard went over the edge of the trail and landed on the side of the mountain about ten feet down.

Celia and the kids raced to the edge and looked over, seeing a huge mound that they assumed was Richard. They waited a breathless moment for any indication of Richard's condition.

In the quietness of the mountain they finally heard a small, distant voice. "I'm all right. I'm *all* right."

Jenna, Kevin, and Celia looked at each other. A second later they burst out laughing. The moment was too funny. Celia pulled out her camera and began snapping pictures. The mound moved. Richard sat in the cold snow and took off his skis. Putting them on his shoulder, he turned and trudged back up to where Celia and the kids were laughing so hard they had tears in their eyes.

Celia kept taking pictures of Richard's ascent, while laughing. When Richard made it back to the trail, he dropped his skis and stood there, his hands on his hips, looking at them. A grin broke out on his face. "You think this is funny? I'll show you what's funny." He picked up a handful of snow and wiped it in Kevin's face and then Jenna's, as they all continued to laugh.

Seeing Celia recording everything in pictures, he made an especially large snowball and went after her. She squealed and tried to get away, but the skis slowed her up. Richard grabbed her and pushed the snow in her face and down her back as they both fell to the ground. Richard's arms were still around her as the laughter stopped. A moment of tenderness passed between them.

Jenna and Kevin looked at each other with hopefulness in their eyes.

The moment was gone as Richard stood and went back to get his skis. Celia was left to get a grip on her ski poles. And on her emotions.

Approaching the exit from the chairlift the next time, Richard and Kevin were both nervous. After reviewing instructions, they got ready to get off. When the time came, Kevin planted his skis, got his balance, and smoothly slid away. Richard was so excited that he cheered. Unfortunately, in the process, he hit a bump and lost his balance, tumbling right in front of the lift. The chairlift stopped. Smiling, Kevin reached out his hand to help his dad up. "It's okay, Dad. You've got to pay attention to what's important. Right?"

"Right," Richard said as they skied off, thinking his son was probably wiser than he knew.

Stopping at noon for lunch, Lila walked into the lodge. She grabbed a tray and filling it with a cup of hot soup, a salad, and coffee, she headed to find a seat. As she looked around, her eyes met Dan's. He was sitting at a table, pad and pen in front of him, watching her, a wide smile on his face. She walked over and sat. "What are you smiling at?"

"Didn't you go out with a black snowsuit this morning?"

"Yes, why?"

Chuckling he said, "Well, it's magically turned white." His laughter grew as Lila looked down to see that she was completely covered with snow from head to toe.

She laughed with him. "At least I'm brave enough to actually get out there and try to ski. Unlike some people," she smirked as she took a sip of her hot coffee.

"I'm working," Dan protested. "I've got a story to write before I head to Florida for Christmas—Florida, a place that caters to my belief that the holidays should be spent wearing shorts and relaxing in the sun."

"I guess. So how does this place rate?" Lila was really interested to know.

"Not bad. They have everything pretty well organized. Enough employees to help with food, souvenirs, chairlift. How was the wait in the rental office?"

Lila paused with her soupspoon halfway to her mouth. He was asking for her opinion. She couldn't help but be thrilled. "It was good. Of course we were there at seven thirty. They got us in and out so that we could be at the chairlift when it opened. I couldn't say how the line is right now."

Dan was quickly writing down the information that Lila gave him. Just to be difficult, she said, "Am I going to get credit for my input?"

Grinning, Dan said, "If you'd like I can add your name as a corroborating source. How's that?" Lila nodded enthusiastically.

"Say, did you see where Sam and Eldon went?" Lila asked.

"Yeah. They headed to the childcare center. They were going to dress up in holiday costumes and entertain the kids today."

Lila smiled. "I can't wait to tell the kids back at the inn." She looked up at the question in Dan's eyes. "They think Sam is Santa Claus and Eldon is his elf."

"Really?" Dan thought. "Yeah, I could see that. Listen, I have to run," he said as he grabbed his pad and pen and stood. "I've got to check out how things are at lunchtime." As an afterthought, he said, "Hey. You didn't let me buy you that drink last night. How about tonight?"

Enjoying the twinkle in his eyes, Lila said, "We'll see." Watching him walk away, she couldn't help letting out one long sigh of female appreciation.

That afternoon, Joe picked up Mary and Bradley from their errands in town and headed to the ski resort to pick up the others. Before five minutes had passed, Bradley was sound asleep, tired out after spending the day in town with his mother. The silence in the van was stifling. All Mary could think about was the embarrassing scene from last night. After taking a walk to cool down, she had come back to the kitchen to find that Joe had finished all the cleaning. She had thanked him at breakfast and he had shrugged it off. Mary still felt that she needed to apologize for Bradley's matchmaking.

Taking a breath for courage, Mary said, "Did you get everything you needed at the hardware store?"

"Yeah. Tom helped me out," he said referring to the storeowner. "He said to bring Bradley in sometime. He wants to show him some magnets they got in."

"That's nice." The mention of Bradley reminded Mary about the previous evening. "Again I want to thank you for cleaning up last night, Joe."

"No problem." Joe was a man of few words.

"I was just so mad with Bradley, I needed to take a walk to calm down."

"I understand."

Sometimes it was like pulling teeth trying to talk to this man. Turning to look at him, Mary said, "I'm really sorry about what Bradley said last night. He embarrassed both of us, and I apologize for him."

"How did he embarrass us, Mary?" Joe asked.

"By insinuating that you and I could . . . you know . . . get together. I mean that's just an impossible idea."

Joe smirked as he looked straight ahead while he drove. He didn't say anything.

"Bradley doesn't realize that you and I are friends and will always be just friends." Joe was quiet. "He doesn't understand that we can't get married just so he can have a father. What a silly idea." Mary was getting progressively uncomfortable. "We're two entirely different people. It would never work out." Irritated by his silence Mary said, "Well, aren't you going to say anything?"

"Sounds to me like you've got everything figured out. I didn't want to interrupt."

Mary thought she detected a trace of offense in his voice. "What was I supposed to tell him?"

"Nothing. Nothing," Joe said as he drove on.

Mary wasn't sure but she felt like she had hurt his feelings in some way. "Joe, I wouldn't hurt you for the world. Tell me what's on your mind."

Joe started to say something, but stopped himself. Tenderly he glanced at Mary. "You've got a good son, there. Don't be so hard on him for wanting a father. I'm really honored that he would think so highly of me."

Before she could think about it, Mary reached over and put her hand on Joe's arm. "He has really good sense." She smiled at him, feeling a warmth flood her body just in sitting next to the man.

He smiled back and Mary thought she saw a yearning, a hunger that echoed in her soul.

"Maybe I could be like his surrogate father," Joe said after a while.

"He'd like that." Shyly, she added, "So would I."

They couldn't see a small grin spread on Bradley's face.

The ride back to the little inn seemed to take forever. The parking lot was jammed with cars and vans trying to get out. Dan was hurriedly writing down his impressions while Lila watched him, moaning from her aches and pains due to her first day of skiing. Genevieve was asleep, as were Sam and Eldon. Jenna and Kevin were tired and hungry, not a good combination for children. They were irritable and kept whining to their parents about the least little thing.

Bradley picked up on this theme and kept asking his mom and Joe how long before supper. Mary was extremely glad that she had set the Crockpot on that morning. Everything would be ready to go when they got back. If they ever got back.

Finally the traffic began to move out onto the highway. It was still crowded, but at least they were moving. When they drove into the long driveway that led to the inn, the sun was setting behind the mountains, causing shadows to cover the land. Joe drove to the front steps of the inn and then slammed on the brakes.

Everyone jerked. Looking up they began complaining to Joe. He turned to them and placed a finger over his lips. Pointing out the front window of the car, they all turned and gasped at the sight.

In front of the van looking in at them stood a reindeer.

Chapter Five

The animal was breathtaking. It stood tall and proud, looking at the people in the van as if they fascinated him. No one moved, no one even breathed as they watched the magnificent animal.

To everyone's surprise, Eldon quietly got out and walked around to the reindeer, gently putting out his hand so the animal could sniff. Sam followed him and easily rubbed his hand down the reindeer's back. Joe came next. Sam whispered, "Why don't you go into the barn and bring out some grain. He looks like he might be hungry."

As Joe did this, the others in the van stared in amazement. Dan finally broke the silence by asking, "Has this ever happened before, Mary?"

"Not as long as I've been here. We'll have to ask Angela."

"Can we go see Dasher, Mama?" asked Bradley.

"How do you know it's Dasher? Could be Rudolph," Kevin said joking with the boy.

"No, it couldn't be Rudolph. See its nose? It's not red. It must be Dasher."

Mary said, "Let's wait until Joe gives us the all clear. I'd hate to startle the poor creature."

After the grain was placed in front of "Dasher" Joe went back to the van and told everyone it was okay to get out. The reindeer seemed incredibly domesticated and allowed the children to pet him while Sam, Eldon, and Joe made sure it couldn't hurt them.

The animal was led back to the barn to rest for the night while the others entered the inn and washed up for supper. That night the chatter around the table was all about the reindeer— where he had come from, what he was doing there, was he one of Santa's famous reindeer. Bradley kept glancing at Sam for some kind of sign that it was his.

Dan told them that typically, reindeer existed in the higher regions of Europe and North America. It was almost impossible that one would wander so far south. Richard pointed out that with the season in full swing the reindeer could have gotten lost from some kind of visiting exhibition.

The children exchanged happy, secretive looks, knowing that whatever the reason, magical things were happening.

Jenna and Kevin went to bed early that evening, Celia's prediction of their exhaustion coming to fruition. While she decided to have a long, hot bath, Richard headed for the lounge.

The inn's lounge featured dark wood paneling on all the walls, giving it a warm, classic vibe. A few small tables with chairs were scattered about. The stools at the bar, in dark leather, stood gleaming, waiting for thirsty travelers. The fireplace was ablaze, as it always was at this time of evening, and the television was turned quietly onto the sports channel.

Joe stood behind the bar mixing drinks and watching a hockey game. He enjoyed this time of the evening when he could watch some sports and listen to the low chatter of the guests. They normally left him alone.

Richard and Dan sat at the bar, each nursing a drink and watching the game. Then Genevieve walked into the room. She had changed into a cocktail dress the shade of forest green. The dress clung to all her curves, causing the men's tongues to hang out. She fluttered her eyelashes and swung back her fiery red hair as she jumped onto a stool. "How about a drink, barkeep?" she asked Joe.

Smiling at her, Joe said, "What'll it be?"

"I'd love a gin and tonic. If it wouldn't be too much trouble," she purred.

"No problem at all, pretty lady," Joe returned.

Mary was livid. She had just walked into the lounge with clean dishtowels in time to hear the two flirt with each other. Well, if that man thought that she was going to let him flirt with a guest under her nose, then he had another thing coming.

"There you go, honey," Joe said as he put the drink in front of Genevieve.

"I'd like one of those, also," said Celia as she walked into the room. Sitting a couple of seats down from Richard, she gave Joe a big smile.

"Another gorgeous woman. Absolutely," he said and began making her a drink.

"Excuse me," Lila shyly said as she sat down next to Dan. "Is that offer for a drink still on?"

Grinning, Dan turned to Lila. "It sure is. Just tell my friend Joe here what's your pleasure." Dan was obviously a few drinks ahead of her.

Looking up at Joe, Lila said, "Could I have a glass of white wine, please?"

"Coming right up." As he went to work on the drinks, Joe said, "My, my, but I am surrounded by lovely ladies tonight."

The drawer for the clean towels slammed shut. Joe quickly looked around to see Mary glaring at him. "Mary, I didn't hear you come in."

"No, I guess you didn't." Why would he have included her in the group of lovely ladies? "I'll be in the kitchen if I'm needed." With that she walked off fuming.

Flirting. He was flirting with other women. Well, why not, the logical part of Mary's brain told her. *He's a red-blooded male. He has needs, desires. You've made it plain that you're not interested. Why shouldn't he look elsewhere for companionship? But not with a guest and not under my roof.* Being honest with herself, she knew she really meant not in front of her. But why did it hurt to see him interested in other women? She

64

didn't even want to think about the answer to that question.

Back at the bar, things were heating up. Richard had moved to a stool next to Genevieve and they were chatting in low voices. Outraged, Joe had taken it upon himself to stand by Celia and engage her in conversation, which was one thing he did not like to do. The jerk, Joe thought. A beautiful wife and kids and he was throwing it away on a plastic woman.

"Joe, another round for Genevieve and me," Richard called.

"Coming up." Joe looked to see Celia looking down into her drink, hiding her pain.

"I think I'll turn in for the night. Thanks for the drink, Joe. And the conversation." Head held high, Celia walked out of the lounge and up the stairs. Joe's heart went out to her. He was so angry with Richard that he was tempted to spit in his drink. Only the call of Dan at the other end of the bar kept him from doing just that.

"Joe, more drinks. We need more drinks. What's the matter, honey, you're not finishing your wine. Would you like something stronger?"

"No, thank you. I'm not much of a drinker. This is all I want."

Dan's voice was getting louder. "Joe, nothing for the lady but I would like another one. And make this one a double."

Joe stood in front of Dan. "Are you sure you want another one?"

"Now Joe. Don't make me put down in my article that the bartender is uncooperative. I'm fine. Anyway, I don't have to drive anywhere, do I?"

With a shake of his head, Joe went back to making Dan's drink.

"Now, where was I? Oh, yeah. I was going to tell you how sexy you looked tonight."

Lila's eyes widened. She looked down at her beige wool pants and white silk shirt. "Thank you." Did Daniel Hamilton just call her sexy?

"You sure look different from high school. I remember you used to wear those dark-rimmed glasses, the big kind that hid your face. You were so quiet, hardly anyone knew you were around."

A slight pain in her stomach took root. She remembered those days. High school had been horrible for her.

Dan took her hand and began to caress it between his. "Yes sir, you're a beautiful woman now."

Lila couldn't help it. She was drawn to him, even knowing that he had had too much to drink. The crooked grin on his face, his laughing green eyes, and his wavy dark brown hair all combined to hypnotize her. Just like it did a long time ago.

Dan leaned forward and kissed her cheek, just a whisper of a kiss, but it sent streams of electricity running up and down her spine. Moving to her neck, dropping little kisses Dan said, "I never realized how sweet you were." Lila was in Heaven. "If I had known it then, I never would have played that trick on you."

Lila froze. To her shame, all the memories she'd suppressed for years came tumbling back.

She had been Dan's tutor through classical literature class. If he didn't pass the class, he couldn't play football, so the teacher had asked Lila to help him out. She had fallen instantly in love with the dashing football star. He was confident, funny, popular, all the things Lila was not. And he had seemed to show genuine interest in her, asking her questions about herself and listening to her answers.

Just before the end of the semester, she received a note, supposedly from Dan. It told of his love for her, but he couldn't think about it until after the classical literature final exam. Lila remembered how her heart had soared after reading the note. She remembered the giddiness she'd felt. If she had been on a rooftop, she would have shouted. She was sure she could have flown.

Through a lot of work, mostly on her part, Dan had passed the class. In a bold move she asked Dan about the note and he told her it had been a joke. His buddies wanted to make sure the tutor was motivated to get him through the class. The jerk even had the audacity to laugh about it. "Gee, I hope it didn't hurt your feelings. You know there could never be anything between us, don't you?"

She had agreed and left hurriedly before the dam in her eyes burst.

Now she had the mighty Dan Hamilton nibbling on her ear. As petty as it seemed, she couldn't let go of the past. Not without an apology or at least an "I was stupid" admission.

Lila cleared her throat and said, "Dan, I don't think we should be doing this here."

"You're right, baby. Why don't you come on up to my room. We can be more comfortable."

Lila wasn't aroused. She wasn't tempted. She was disillusioned. "I don't think that's a very wise thing to do."

"Maybe not, but it sure could be fun." Dan felt Lila tense and looked into her eyes. "No? You're turning me down?"

With eyes of pain, Lila looked at Dan as she felt not only sorry for the lonely high school girl but also for the man she was looking at. He was a shell. No substance, a mere shadow of a human, someone who thought of no one but himself. "Yes, I guess I am."

Dan turned back to his drink. He took a big swig and chuckled. "I guess we were right about you back in high school." Lila knew she should have left but she had to stay, just as a moth approaching the flame, she had to hear the worst from Dan. "The guys and I thought you were a prude, all brains, nothing else going on. No sparkle, no passion, no life. We used to laugh at what kissing you must feel like. Maybe like kissing my old Aunt Harriet."

He now looked down at Lila's body. "You have filled out a little but I bet you're as cold as the ice on the pond. Well, babe, if I want a chill I can always take a cold shower." He threw back his drink and added the death knell to Lila's esteem.

"I suppose I knew it back then. No sparks, no chemistry, nothing between us." Words from her past that now came back to haunt her. Dan stood, settled up with Joe and headed to his room.

Lila was frozen on her stool. Her eyes looked out but all she saw was the failure she had become as a woman. She saw her life ahead—a spinster teacher with no one except a cat for company—a lonely, depressing existence.

Joe whispered, "Lila, can I help you?"

Hearing the voice as if from afar, she shook her head. On automatic pilot, Lila stood and slowly walked to the stairway and upstairs to her room. She waited until she locked the door and changed into pajamas before she succumbed to the misery. With the lights off and the covers pulled over her, she began to weep. Her tears were bitter as she saw herself through the eyes of men.

She didn't like what she saw. Her quiet moans of sadness echoed the sad sound of the wind that swirled around the inn. And she cried for the loneliness of it all.

"I don't think we're supposed to be in here," Jenna told Bradley and her brother the next morning.

"It's okay. Dasher's had breakfast, he doesn't mind if we pay him a visit."

The reindeer had been put in a small pen in the barn. Telephone calls to see if anyone knew about a missing reindeer had turned up nothing. Already "Dasher" as he was called was making himself at home at the inn and seemed content enough to let the humans care for him.

Kevin patted Dasher on the back, enjoying the soft feel of his skin. "Sometimes I wish I could be a big animal." Bradley and Jenna looked at him. "I mean, what does he have to worry about?" They all thought about it for a minute.

"Mom and Dad were angry with each other again this morning," Jenna said.

"I think it had something to do with Ginger," Kevin said.

"Who's Ginger?" Bradley asked.

"Have you ever seen the show *Gilligan's Island*?" When Bradley shook his head Kevin continued. "It's about seven people who are shipwrecked on an island out in the ocean. One of the people is a red-haired girl who thinks she's God's gift to the world. Just like . . ."

Bradley laughed. "Oh, you mean Miss St. Clair. Mom says she needs a lesson in thinking of others." Looking quickly at Jenna and Kevin he said, "I'm not supposed to tell anyone that."

"Don't worry, Bradley, we won't tell. Anyway, we think Mom and Dad are fighting because of her." Jenna sighed. "And they were starting to like each other again."

Bradley let out a long-suffering sigh. "Yeah, Mom and Joe wouldn't even look at each other at breakfast. She was madder than when I threw my ball through the window."

"And did you see Miss Lila this morning? She had puffy eyes. I think she'd been crying. She left the table when Mr. Hamilton came down."

Angry, Kevin said, "What's going on here? I thought this was Christmas, the time of 'Peace on

Earth, Goodwill to all men'? All I see are adults fighting and arguing and us kids get stuck in the middle of it all."

"It's a shame, isn't it?" The kids turned to see Sam walking into the barn. "You're right, Kevin. Christmas is about hope. It's about new life, new chances, not the death of dreams."

"I'm sorry, Sam, but I don't think I can keep believing." Kevin felt good to be able to say it out loud.

"I don't blame you, Kevin. But along with wishing and believing, sometimes it takes a little involvement."

"What does that mean?" Kevin asked.

"It means we need to be active in helping the wish come true." The kids' eyes widened with interest. "What we need here is a plan."

"What about Miss Lila? She's part of this," Jenna said.

"Absolutely. Miss Lila is even now working on her own plan. But we'll include her in ours. It never hurts to have more people on your team." Sam smiled a bright smile at the children and walked over to pet the reindeer. "Right, Dasher?"

Dasher grunted his approval.

Dan felt awful. His eyes were bloodshot, his head was pounding, and his guilt was so heavy he felt like he was already six feet under. He sat in the parlor with a cup of strong coffee, his eyes closed, relaxing in an easy chair as Christmas music quietly filled the air.

Angela came rushing in with two aspirin and a glass of water. "Here you go, Mr. Hamilton," she said in a soft voice. "Can I get you an ice pack?"

Dan lifted one eye to Angela. "How did you know . . .?"

"It's a small inn. I figured you needed a little mothering after last night." She handed him the aspirin and instead of leaving him to die in his misery, sat next to him. "Honestly, I've never been able to figure out the attraction of hard liquor. Does it really help you feel good?" Before Dan had an opportunity to answer, Angela did. "No. It only clouds your judgment and makes you feel like death warmed over the next day."

"Angela." He struggled with the words as his mouth felt like dried up, stale cotton. "Do you know where Lila is? I have to talk to her."

Smiling, Angela said, "I'm sure she'll be here soon." She patted his knee. "I'm also sure that she'd understand if you'd like to explain things to her."

Dan looked up at Angela. "How do you know . . . Never mind. I guess everyone must know what an idiot I am."

"You know, Mr. Hamilton. Dan. I think you're a very intelligent man. You know what you need to do."

Sighing heavily Dan said, "Last night in my inebriated state, I said some things to Lila. Hurtful things, stupid things. Things I didn't mean. She should hate me."

"Lila's a very kind person, Dan. Like I said, I'm sure she'll understand."

Dan took the aspirin and drank the water. He smiled warmly at Angela. "Thank you."

"Angela, that book isn't in the library. Are you sure . . ." Lila stopped dead in her tracks when she saw Dan looking up at her. "Oh, I'm sorry." She turned to leave the room.

"Ah, yes. Pride and Prejudice. I guess I was mistaken. It's probably in here. Why don't you have a look around?" Angela stood, gave Dan an encouraging nod, and left.

Lila walked to the bookshelves and began to quickly look for the book she wanted to read.

"Lila."

She didn't answer so with great effort, he repeated, "Lila."

"Hmm?" She didn't turn but kept looking at the books.

Dan moaned as he rose and looked at the books with her. "What are we looking for?"

"Pride and Prejudice. By Jane Austen."

"Yeah, I know who wrote Pride and Prejudice." After a breath he said, "Lila, I need to talk to you."

"I think you've said enough."

"Here it is," Dan said, pulling out the novel.

"Great. Let me have it." Lila took hold of the book but Dan wouldn't let go of it. "If you don't mind, I'd like to have the book, please."

"Not until you let me apologize for last night."

Her brows lifted, as if she was surprised. "All right," she said folding her arms across her chest. "Go ahead."

Dan was a little shaky on his legs. "No, let's sit down," he said as he led her to one of the sofas. She sat up straight while he collapsed against the cushions. Moaning he said, "Lila, never, and I mean never drink as much as I did last night."

"Well, it's not the best apology I've ever heard but I suppose it's the best you can do. Now may I have my book please?"

Confused, Dan said, "No. Wait. That wasn't an apology."

"Oh, already backing out of it?" Lila taunted.

"Listen, would you wait just a second so I can catch my breath and feel like I don't want to puke all over you?" Dan breathed in and out several times. "I am very sorry for all that I said and did last night. I was terrible to you and I deeply regret it." Dan took another big breath. "Was that apology good enough for you?"

She took a moment. "Okay, apology accepted. Could I have my book please?"

"Really, Lila. I'm sorry. I didn't mean what I said last night. It was the alcohol talking."

Lila smiled without any humor. "Sure. My book?"

Dan frowned. "Lila. We've been friends for a long time. It would mean a lot to me if you accepted my apology."

"Friends? Really? Okay Dan, fine. Whatever. Apology accepted," she said sharply before grabbing the book and walking out of the parlor.

Dan watched her go and felt a load of guilt that made his headache feel like nothing. Somehow he would find a way to make it up to Lila. He had to. He needed a friend. Especially with what he was dealing with.

Chapter Six

Mary didn't understand why she was so cross. She had been reasoning with herself ever since the night before trying to make some sense of her feelings for Joe.

Her conclusion was she shouldn't have any.

The big shed behind the kitchen housed all the outdoor equipment and since she was going to be leading a group of cross-country skiers that afternoon, that was where she was, going over her checklist. All the cross-country skis, boots, bindings, and poles hung neatly against the wall, clean and polished, ready to go. As she quietly worked, the door to the shed opened and Joe stepped in.

Obviously feeling a bit uncomfortable being there with her, he said, "Sorry. I'll just get my gear and get out of your way. Unless you need any help."

"Nope. I'm fine," Mary said not even looking up at him.

He grabbed his things and started to leave but hesitated. "Mary, is something wrong?"

"Why should anything be wrong?"

"Well, because you've been as cranky as an old bear this morning."

"Thank you."

"I don't mean to be unkind. You've been harsh with Bradley, you haven't looked at me. It's not like you. If something's wrong, you can talk to me about it." He added in a low voice, "That is, unless it's woman stuff and then maybe Angela would be a better choice." Joe's face started to blush.

Mary couldn't help it. She started to giggle. Here was this big, strong man and he disintegrated at the thought of "woman stuff." Mary looked up at him, glimpsing that hard, thin face of his, the face she had grown accustomed to seeing every day, the face that now haunted her dreams. She slowly walked forward and in a rare show of emotion, gently touched his cheek with her fingertips.

"Joe. I'm sorry for my behavior. You're right. I haven't been myself since yesterday." She smiled and turned back to her clipboard. "Thanks for making me laugh. I really needed that."

Clearly confused, Joe said, "Okay." As he started to go he said, "Since I'll be bringing up the rear on the cross-country skiing group, is there anything I should know?"

"No," Mary said. "Well, perhaps I should tell you it's probably not a good idea to flirt with the guests on the trail." She was uncomfortable bringing it up but believed they should be clear about that.

He appeared to have been registered speechless. When he found his voice, he said, "What are you talking about?"

Pretending to be working down her checklist Mary said, "I know that you're a healthy man and have . . . needs. You were flirting with the women in the lounge last night," she said and added too quickly, "Although it's probably not my place to say anything about it. I just think the women need to be paying attention to their skiing this afternoon instead of exchanging glances with you."

He looked at her with his mouth open, his mind obviously swirling. She would have paid good money to know what he was thinking. She didn't have to wait long.

Joe dropped his equipment and walked over to her, firmly taking her shoulders and waiting. When she did, he stared into her eyes. She couldn't think, couldn't move.

Holding her gaze, he slowly lowered his head. The touch of their lips meeting sent jolts of electricity running through her body. When she shuddered, he pulled her closer. He rubbed his lips across hers before ending the kiss. The contact had only been a few seconds but she felt eons had passed.

The moment was so beautiful, she didn't want to open her eyes. His hands rubbed her shoulders and softly, he said, "I wasn't flirting with those women. I was only trying to be kind. Nothing more. Got it?"

Mary's head bobbled as her eyes opened. She looked at the large, sensitive man holding her shoulders and a rush of emotion flooded her. Could she ever go back to just being co-workers, even just friends with this man? In a soft breath she said, "Joe—"

He stopped her with a finger over her lips. "You have to get ready for the group and I have a couple of things to do before we go. Not now." With a grin, he backed away, retrieved his gear, and left.

Leaving Mary standing there, still feeling his lips on hers. Reveling in the feeling that Joe had kissed her. Glory be!

Back in the barn, Sam and Bradley waited. Eldon stood nearby, silently grooming the reindeer. When Joe came in he said, "Here's my ski equipment, Sam. What did you want to know about it?"

The glow of happiness on Joe's face told Sam all he wanted to know. He looked at Bradley and winked. Bradley grinned. Since he had sent Joe into the shed after seeing Mary go in there, Sam figured he should play out the act. "Tell me all about the equipment you use to go cross-country skiing."

As if he didn't already know.

The little group met in the back of the inn for the cross-country lesson and outing. Mary stood in front with all the equipment waiting for everyone to arrive. When she saw Joe, she fumbled with her skis dropping them at her feet.

Joe smiled inwardly at her reaction. He enjoyed the fact that the kiss had affected her as much as him.

"Let's see. We've got Dan, Lila, Richard, Celia, Jenna, Kevin." Mary looked up from her clipboard. "Has anyone seen Genevieve?"

Kevin piped up. "She's not coming."

"Are you sure?"

"He's right. Sam and Eldon borrowed the van to take her into town to do some shopping," Joe said.

Jenna and Kevin exchanged looks, smiled, and gave each other a fist pump.

After explaining the basics of the sport, Mary and Joe helped everyone get into their gear. They practiced going back and forth across the yard for a while before they were ready to head out on the trail.

"You okay, Mom?" Kevin asked as they started to line up.

"Oh don't worry about your mom. She's always been an exceptional athlete," Richard said with a grin.

"Why, thank you, Richard. I hope my body agrees with you." Celia took her place in line.

Richard had gotten behind the kids who were behind Celia but Kevin said, "Dad, do you mind if Jenna and I get in front of Mom?"

"Why?" he asked.

Let's see. Why, why, why. "Because we wanted to be closer to the front. You know, in case Mrs. Michaels gives out instructions."

"Oh, okay." Jenna and Kevin moved ahead of Celia. She looked back at Richard with her eyebrows raised. He shrugged back. As they started out, Richard looked in front of him to see that he had a delightful view of Celia's backside. Memories pulled him back in time as he remembered that derrière. His body began to ache. It was going to be a long afternoon.

The line of skiers headed out slowly. It was a lovely winter day. The sun was shining brightly, causing the ice on the tree branches to appear as flickering diamonds. Everyone was having a good time. Mary headed up the line, followed by Lila, then Dan, Jenna, Kevin, Celia, Richard, and finally Joe. Even with a few tumbles, the group enjoyed the sport and the camaraderie of being together.

They stopped at the end of the trail to sit and rest. Mary pulled out granola bars and raisin boxes from her backpack. Joe pulled out water bottles from his. Everyone found a place to sit on logs arranged for just such a break. The Davis family sat together, the kids in the middle and a parent on each side. Celia and Richard were polite but not overly interested in each other, to the kids' chagrin.

Joe offered Mary a water bottle. "It's going well, isn't it?"

"Yes, it is." She tried not to let her heart beat too fast at his nearness.

"What's Bradley doing this afternoon?" Joe asked.

"He and Angela are baking Christmas cookies. He said he wanted to put walnuts and raisins in them because they're your favorite. Is that right?"

He smiled. "Yes."

"Well, why didn't you say so? I would have been making more cookies with walnuts and raisins if I'd've known that."

Joe lifted his fingers to Mary's hair. He stroked the auburn strands that hung below her woolen hat. "Would you have, Mary?" he asked in a low, hypnotizing voice.

"Yes," she whispered to him, meeting his eyes. Ever since being with him in the shed, Mary had been thinking about that kiss. Her knees would weaken as she replayed the whole scene in her mind. Looking into Joe's eyes now, she knew how badly she wanted another kiss. And another. And not just tender kisses, but passionate kisses. Just the thought made her heart race and her breath quicken.

Apparently Joe wanted the same thing. She saw the hungry look on his face and was excited at the possibilities. She knew she probably shouldn't encourage it but she'd been alone for so long and it felt so good to have this man that she admired, that she was crazy about, pay her a little attention. Before too long she would have to confide to him her past. He needed to know before he continued, thinking there might be a future for them.

"Hey, Mrs. Michaels, could I have another granola bar?" Kevin's request had them pulling back, mentally returning to the group.

"Of course, honey. Let me get you one," Mary said, her face showing a faint shade of pink.

Kevin got his bar and sat back down next to his dad.

"Genevieve didn't say anything to me about going shopping. I wonder why she decided not to come?" Richard asked Kevin.

Being particularly interested in his granola bar, Kevin just shrugged. "They must be having a sale, or something. You know how girls are."

"Hey!" Celia and Jenna said in unison and smiled at each other.

"I just mean, last night she said she was looking forward to this outing." Richard thought about it. "You kids didn't say anything to her that would make her not want to come, did you?"

"Really, Richard. Don't blame the kids if your girlfriend has better things to do with her time than go cross-country skiing with you," Celia said.

Richard bristled. "I just don't want the kids to think they can be rude to anyone that . . . they shouldn't be rude to anyone, that's all."

"Not all women choose the big outdoors over a shopping village." Smiling down at her daughter, Celia added, "Jenna and I are unique."

With a grin Richard said, "You two are that." He took another swallow of water. Thinking aloud he said, "But it sure must have been some kind of sale."

Kevin and Jenna looked at each other and smiled.

Dan got his snack and walked to where Lila sat. Sitting next to her, he offered a shy smile. "Is it all right if I sit here, Lila?" he asked.

"Sure," she replied. She noticed that his eyes had cleared some. However, they still showed traces of a miserable hangover. What had she seen in him? He was nothing but a drinking, carousing, shallow human being. Definitely not what she wanted in her life.

"How do you like cross-country skiing?" Dan asked.

"I love it. It's so much fun. Mary is a good teacher. I think I've only fallen once or twice."

Dan chuckled. "Yes. It's a pretty good trail. You've taken to the sport really well."

"Thanks," Lila said, not wanting to allow him any entrance into her mind.

They ate in silence, listening to the quiet around them, occasionally broken by the kids talking with their parents.

Not wanting to endure his company any longer, Lila said, "Well, I think I'll stretch until we're ready to get going again."

"Lila," Dan said grasping her arm. "You're not going to hold last night against me, are you?"

Looking him squarely into the eyes, she said, "I accepted your apology, Dan. I don't plan on being friends with you." She shook off his hand and walked to the edge of the clearing and began stretching exercises.

Dan watched her. There had always been something about Lila. She had an inner strength. He had always admired that. All those years ago when he had been such a supreme jerk and told her that the note had been a joke, she hadn't crumbled, she hadn't cried. She'd stood tall and calmly walked away. He gave her a lot of credit for that. He hated that he had so alienated her from him.

He really could have used a friend.

Once back at the inn, the group dispersed to rest and clean up before dinner. Sam, Eldon, and Genevieve came back and she headed to her room to admire the treasures she'd found in the quaint stores of the village.

In the library, Angela met with Sam and Eldon. Angela had a pot of hot chocolate and sugar cookies set up in front of a roaring fire. They helped themselves and all sat down.

"Tell me how the trip to town went?" Angela asked Sam.

"I don't know, Angela. I don't think she's receptive. Her mind is intent on only pleasing herself. She's going to be a problem."

"I'm afraid she is a problem. But thankfully, I think I've got a solution on the way."

Sam smiled. "Good. How did the cross-country skiing go for everyone?"

Angela looked thoughtful. "Mixed reviews, I'd say. Mary is completely flummoxed right now. Joe is loving it."

"That's good."

"Yes, it is. How they'll handle it is another thing. Your idea about Richard following Celia on the trail was brilliant." Sam gave an appreciative bow. "However, he needs to remember more about why he fell in love with Celia in the first place than how her bottom looks in pants," Angela said as Eldon laughed.

She smirked at him. "And I don't know about Lila. She has every right to be furious with Dan. His little scene with her last night cost her what little self-esteem she had left. She's not letting him get close again."

"Well, I say good for her. It wouldn't hurt to let that buckaroo stew a little bit in the consequences of his actions."

"Normally I'd agree with you. However, Dan got a disturbing phone call last night. It's the reason he was overindulging at the lounge." She put up her hand and said, "I know that's no excuse but it does explain a few things. He's going to need a woman like Lila to help him."

With concern in her eyes, she said, "I'm so thankful the children are drawn to you. How do you think they're doing?"

"Hesitantly optimistic. Bradley is a little trooper. He's so sure that Joe is supposed to be his stepfather that it's easy to work with him. The Davis children are a little harder."

Angela shook her head. "Poor little dears."

"They've had to endure a lot. Belief comes hard for them. I hate to see how they'll react if this doesn't work out."

"Children are incredibly resilient. Unfortunately, they have to be."

Sam lifted his eyebrows. "Any idea if the Davis couple will get back together or not?"

"It's not for me to say. It doesn't effect our helping the children through this time."

"But I worry about their faith if things don't work out the way they wish."

She said, "Just leave that to me. The children will make it just fine. They may have a few tough times yet, but they'll learn how to have faith. And who to have faith in."

"It seems that we're going to need more than a week to help these people straighten out their lives."

Angela grinned widely. Sam and Eldon had seen that smile before. Sam quietly asked, "What have you got in mind?"

She picked up her mug of cocoa and held it up in salute. "Gentlemen, I hope you've packed your long underwear."

Chapter Seven

Dinner was a loud affair, as everyone wanted to talk about the skiing trail or the shopping trip. Angela enjoyed watching the faces of her guests beaming with their accomplishments of the day.

Richard sat between Jenna and Genevieve, splitting his attention between conversations of animals seen on the trail and antiques seen in the stores. When Genevieve shivered, Richard asked, "Are you cold?"

"Yes, I just can't seem to get warm today."

"There's a hot tub out back. How about I meet you there after dinner?"

The totally feminine smile of Genevieve was so provocative it should have been illegal. "I'd love that," she cooed.

Jenna had heard the exchange, as had Sam who sat directly across from Richard. Looking at Jenna's sad eyes, he said, "Hey kids, how about we check in on Dasher after dinner?"

"Sure," they both replied, Jenna showing little enthusiasm.

Lila was lost in her own thoughts. She had had enough of feeling sorry for herself. The tears she had shed overnight would be her last on the matter. After a successful morning planning her future, an invigorating afternoon of cross-country skiing, and a healthy confrontation with Dan, she felt she was ready to visibly repair her self-esteem and move on.

"Celia, Angela mentioned that you sell 'Pretty Lady Cosmetics.'"

"Yes, I do. Is there something I can help you with?" Celia asked as she spooned a bite of chocolate cake into her mouth.

"Yes. I . . . need help." Lila laughed at her own indecision while she toyed with her dessert.

"How about I bring my case over to your room after dinner?"

"That would be great," Lila smiled sincerely.

Richard and Genevieve met in the downstairs hallway leading to the back door. Genevieve wore a long terrycloth robe along with her designer snow boots. Richard wore his jeans over his bathing suit and a sweatshirt, jacket, and boots. Together they headed out into the cold to find the hot tub.

The lights in the backyard cast a dim glow on the hot tub at the back of the property. As they reached the tub, they saw something on the covered top.

"What's that?" Genevieve asked.

"Probably just some debris," he answered. He reached out to clear it away and the pile moved. Genevieve screamed and a small dog quickly moved off the covering and stumbled back toward the barn. Laughing nervously, Richard removed the covering and turned the tub on. The swirling jets came alive and the steam from the water rose above the tub. Yes, sir, this was just what he needed, he thought. If only they had a bottle of wine, it would be perfect. Genevieve started to take off her robe and Richard quickly reached over to help her. The robe gone, she stood there in the smallest string bikini he'd ever seen.

Goose bumps quickly formed on the smooth skin as she chuckled at his expression. "All right. Let's get in before we freeze."

He took off his outer clothes and they eagerly stepped into the water and sank down to find—

It was lukewarm.

They both looked at each other, neither knowing what to say. Finally she said, "Isn't it supposed to be hotter than this?"

"For crying out loud." He glanced over at the water temperature. The reading was ninety degrees. It was lower than their body heat, which obviously was plummeting at this point. "Something must be wrong. We're going to have to get out."

Genevieve stood to get out but quickly dropped back into the water. Her teeth chattered. "It-it-it's freezing out here. How-how are we going to make it back to the inn?"

Richard surveyed the situation. They were wet, outside in the freezing cold temperature. The house was a good hundred yards away. They had no choice. They might catch pneumonia but they had to hurry for the house. "We're going to have to make a run for it. We'll jump out real quick, grab our clothes and run to the house."

"Are you kidding? I'm not going to run barefoot through the snow!"

Richard's mind immediately went back to a winter years ago. He and Celia were at a ski resort in West Virginia. The hot tub was outdoors, surrounded by snow. He had picked up his wife from the bubbling Jacuzzi and dropped her into a bank of snow. She had laughed and thrown a snowball at him before jumping back into the hot tub. For a moment his heart ached as he remembered her laughter.

"Did you hear what I said, Richard?" Genevieve asked.

Coming back to himself, he said, "What?"

"I'm going to put my boots on before running back to the inn. Gee, I hope Mary still has some hot cider. She could probably heat some up for me, right?"

"Sure," he said dryly. "All right, are you ready?" She nodded. "One, two, three, go." The two jumped out and made a quick grab for their clothes, simultaneously trying to step in their boots. Genevieve's foot had trouble slipping into the tiny shoe. Knowing that he shouldn't leave her stranded, Richard stood shivering while she worked her foot in. Finally, she headed to the inn, Richard right behind her.

Once inside the inn, they walked quickly toward the stairs. As he passed the kitchen, Richard could have sworn he heard giggling.

When he had taken a steaming hot shower and changed clothes, he went back out to the hot tub. He didn't want to leave it uncovered, so he carefully lifted the cover and replaced it. A light seemed to be on in the pump house, but he didn't think anything about it.

"Okay, the doctor is in the house," Celia said while rubbing her hands together. The previous night, she had shown Lila all of her goodies from the "Pretty Lady Cosmetic" company. In the early morning light she was ready to make some magic.

Lila sat on the edge of her bed, the "Pretty Lady Cosmetics" case laid out beside her, while Celia analyzed her face.

"Hmm. Your complexion is very nice, Lila. Very smooth. High cheekbones." Celia bent to peer into Lila's eyes. "What color do you call your eyes?"

Lila chuckled. "On my drivers license it says brown. They really change colors depending on what color I'm wearing up around my neck. I think my mood sometimes changes the color, too."

Celia continued to study them. "Fascinating. I've never seen eyes this color before."

"I can believe that," Lila said dryly.

"No, I mean they're beautiful." Celia stood straight. "They're very beautiful, with tinges of gold around the rims." Turning to her case she said, "The only problem is that your eyes seem to be small and recede from your face. You need to highlight them, make them appear bigger."

"And you can do that?"

"Oh, honey. You'd be surprised what a little of my makeup can do. Now sit still, enjoy, and let me work."

Lila laughed. Celia thought her laughter was so sweet. It made her smile. "Tell me more about yourself, Lila. Why did you decide to come here for your vacation?"

"Well, I wanted to get away from the noise of New York. I wanted a place so quiet that I'd be able to think . . . about things."

Celia smiled. "I understand." She took several small containers from her case and held them up. "With your coloring, I think you should stick to earth tones. Since your eyes tend to change colors, you probably don't want to wear bright colors on your eyes like blue or green. They would clash if your eyes turned, say, violet."

Lila giggled. "Earth tones. Gotcha."

As she set to work on Lila's eyes, Celia continued the conversation. "I've enjoyed the quiet here. Although, with the kids it's never quiet. But I really love the beauty all around us, the peacefulness of it all."

"Where are you from?"

"New Rochelle, New York. We wanted to live in a nice town for families. Richard works in

New York and . . ." Celia's expression darkened. Her eyes lowered as she turned back to the case supposedly looking for something.

"I'm sorry," Lila said.

Celia tried to shake off the feelings. "No, don't apologize. I'm trying not to fall apart every time I think about my marriage. Or my divorce." She sighed. "It's still such a strange, depressing feeling, I wonder if it will ever go away." When Lila didn't respond, Celia continued to speak.

"I never expected to be in this position, not in a million years. Richard and I were so in love with each other. We met in college in Rochester." She smiled. "I knew when I first saw him. He was the most handsome man I had ever met, so funny, so interesting. We dated our last two years and married after graduation."

"Go on," Lila said when she hesitated.

"We moved to New York City and set up housekeeping, a tiny little studio on the lower East side. Richard found a job with a big company in the financial district and I worked as an emergency room nurse at New York Downtown Hospital." Sighing, Celia went on. "We didn't have a thing, really, but we were happy as church mice. Richard would bring me a flower, just one flower every so often. He'd kiss me and tell me that one day, we'd have flowers all around our home. Every weekend, we'd splurge by walking through the city and finding a two-dollar treat that we could share."

"That sounds so romantic."

Smiling Celia continued to work on Lila's face. "It was. Richard was always thinking of little things like that to do. He'd leave me notes, write me poems, terrible, awful poems that made me laugh." Celia chuckled at the memories.

"Then about three years into the marriage I got pregnant with Kevin. We were thrilled. Two years later, Jenna came. Richard continued with the company, doing very well and we found a home in New Rochelle."

When Celia reached for a tube and poured out a tiny amount onto her index finger, Lila asked, "What's that?"

"Foundation. You need just a little to even out your tones. I'd suggest medium rose for you."

As Celia smoothed the cream onto Lila's skin, Lila quietly said, "What happened? Do you mind talking about it?"

With a sad smile Celia said, "No. I guess it's what happens with so many marriages. I got involved with the P.T.A. and Richard got involved with his career. We were both so busy we never had time to just be a couple." Celia was quiet for a moment. "I think Richard fell out of love with me and into love with the city and all it offers. I'm just not . . . well, exciting enough for him anymore."

"But that's not true." Lila looked up at Celia. "You've been downhill skiing, you've been cross-country skiing. You're going ice skating today. I think you're very adventurous."

"Maybe. But I'm not enough." When Lila started to protest, Celia jumped in. "That's just the way it is. I've accepted it." Her brow furrowed when she added, "Now if I could get the kids to accept it."

"It's hard on children. They love both parents. They want them to be together."

Celia looked at Lila, "That's right, you're a teacher, aren't you?"

"Yes. Second grade. I see kids going through divorce all the time. My heart always goes out to them."

Celia thought about this. "Listen. Could you maybe spend a little time with Kevin and Jenna? See how they're coping, what they're thinking?"

"I don't know if I can help, Celia."

"I just want to know how they're doing, that's all. Richard and I suspect that the reason they wanted this vacation was to get us back together. I don't know how to deal with the disappointment they'll have when we go back home. Maybe you could sort of ease the way."

"Oh, Celia." When she gave Lila her most hopeful look, the woman finally said, "I'll see what I can do."

"Thanks." Putting her sponge down, Celia stood straight and said, "Okay, gorgeous. Time to look in the mirror."

Lila walked over to the dresser mirror and looked, Celia behind her. Lila's hair, long and shiny framed a face she obviously was surprised to see. Her eyes shone brightly, highlighting a delicate oval face with exotic cheekbones. Lila's generous lips curved up and her eyes sparkled. "That's me?" she asked with a squeak in her voice.

"I love this part of the job. That's you. You're a vision, Lila." She hugged the still stunned woman and whispered in her ear, "Dan Hamilton's not going to be able to keep his eyes off you."

Lila looked at Celia. "Oh, I'm not doing this to get his attention. We're not even friends anymore," she said, unable to keep the pain out of her voice.

"What happened?"

Lila walked to Celia's case to help her put things back. "As you probably heard, we knew each other from high school. Not very well, he was the popular football player and I was the brain that helped him pass his lit class. It's a familiar story. I had a crush on him, he couldn't be bothered with me."

Celia walked next to Lila. "But you're not in high school anymore."

"No, but some things don't change. I came here to think about my life. Think about where I wanted to go from here. I'm ready to take a few more risks but Dan Hamilton is not a risk I want to take." Her eyes met Celia's. "It hurts the heart too much."

She took Lila's arm. "I understand, honey. It's your life. You're entitled to live it any way you see fit." Grinning, she linked arms with Lila and said, "Now, you'll be beautiful doing it."

"Well, look at the two of you," Angela said when Celia and Lila came late to breakfast. As the others devoured their plates of French toast, she

97

chuckled and added, "We're waiting for you like pigs at the trough."

Dan and Richard both looked up to see the women entering. Richard smiled at the satisfied look on Celia's face. Then went back to eating his breakfast.

Dan was entranced. He stood and after Lila helped her plate, pulled out a chair for her. "Good morning, beautiful."

Without a glance at him, Lila took the chair and muttered, "Good morning."

Joe came out of the kitchen with a fresh batch of toast. He wore an expression of deep concern as he set the food on the buffet.

"How's the weather reports looking, Joe?" Angela asked.

"Not good." He walked over to look out a window. "The clouds aren't bad right now, but the wind is moving in from the north. Looks like a big storm coming in from Canada."

"Really?" Kevin said. "Do you think we could get snowed in?"

"Of course not, son. Now, finish your breakfast so we can go build that snowman you wanted."

Turning back to Angela, Joe said, "I'm going into the village today to get a couple of things, make sure we're stocked up when it hits."

"Why don't you take Mary with you?" Angela said. "She may need to pick up a few things also."

Joe agreed. "That's a good idea. But I don't know what she'll—"

"Let Bradley stay here with us," Sam said. "We'll all go make snowmen this morning." Jenna and Kevin cheered.

"All right. We'll leave right after breakfast. If the weather holds, we'll still plan to do some ice skating at the pond this afternoon." More cheers from the kids.

After Joe left to confer with Mary, Jenna looked up at her dad. "This is the best vacation ever." With the joy she felt, she wrapped her arms around his middle and hugged tightly. "Thank you, Daddy."

His voice heavy with emotion, Richard said, "You're welcome, Pumpkin." He looked around at the table to find everyone grinning at him. Everyone, that is, except Genevieve who wasn't paying any attention. She was busy scraping off the powdered sugar from her French toast.

The snow was just right for building snowmen. Richard had Jenna and Kevin busy building a whole army of them. Jenna had begged her mother to join them but after breakfast she said she had a few things to do and would be out later to see their work.

Mary bundled Bradley up so tight in his snowsuit that he could hardly move. He looked like the Michelin tire man coming into the yard. Kevin couldn't help giggling. As soon as Joe and Mary left for Stowe Village, Sam took off the extra mittens, the extra cap, and the extra scarf that Mary had tied on the young boy. "Mothers are like that, Bradley. But sometimes they just don't know how hardy we men are."

"Yeah!" Bradley growled like a bear. Kevin and Jenna laughed.

The laughter stopped when Genevieve appeared at the back porch. "Richard. I was going to go for a little walk and was wondering if you'd like to join me?" The edges of her mouth lifted and her eyes got real wide. The kids rolled their eyes at each other.

Richard hesitated. "Well, I promised the kids I'd build snowmen with them right now."

"But you're ice skating with them later. And look, Sam is here with them. He'll babysit for you, won't you, Sam?"

Kevin was close to forgetting all the manners his mother had taught him. Babysit him? What was he, an infant? His dad just couldn't leave them to go with her, could he?

"If that's what Mr. Davis wants," Sam said looking squarely at Richard.

Richard looked over at his kids. Kevin's eyes were hard as he looked down. Jenna's eyes were pleading as they pierced his heart. This was hard on his kids, he knew that. He didn't want to make it harder. "Maybe later," he smiled at Genevieve.

Heaving a dramatic sigh, she said, "Well, all right."

"Hey, why don't you help us? We're going to build a whole village of people," Richard said.

Genevieve chortled. "I don't think so. Building snow people really isn't my thing." With a brief intense look at Richard, she said, "*Ciao, darling*," and left on her solitary walk.

Kevin and Jenna both breathed a sigh of relief.

"Mr. Davis, you know I thought I saw some tools for building snowmen in the shed. Maybe you'd like to take a glance and see if you can find them," Sam said.

"Okay." Richard stood, brushing the snow off his pants. "Kids, I'll be right back."

When he was out of earshot, Sam said, "All right, is everyone clear about the ice skating this afternoon? All three heads nodded. You're going to have to be on your best behavior, make everything nice for the adults."

"Do you really think it's going to help?" Jenna asked.

Sam pondered that. "Well, it couldn't hurt, now could it?"

Kevin said, "Gee, I was afraid Dad was going to leave. That was a close one. I don't want Dad taking a walk with 'Ginger.'"

"Me either," Jenna agreed.

"Who's 'Ginger'?" asked Sam.

Bradley spoke up. "That's what we call the red-haired lady on account of she's like Ginger from that show Gibby's Island."

"No, it's *Gilligan's Island*," Kevin corrected.

Sam thought about that for a moment and let out with a guffaw so loud and so long that tears were streaming down his face. "I can't think of a better name for her," he said between laughing fits. The kids laughed with him.

"Hey kids, look what I found?" Richard said excitedly as he rushed back from the shed. In one hand he held a bucket with small trowels, pieces of coal, buttons, and assorted old scarves and hats. In the other hand was a small sled. The kids ran over to see the bright red riding device.

"Oh, yeah. I forgot that was there," Bradley said.

"Well, how about we give it a try?" Richard asked to the squeals of the children. They walked over to a small hill leading into a large pasture and set the sled on the snow.

"Show us how, Daddy," Jenna said.

Richard looked to Sam who indicated with his outstretched arm, "You first." He swallowed hard, and mounted the sled. The kids joyously gave him a push and watched as he glided down the incline, hooting and hollering.

Sam laughed as the three kids raced down the hill to congratulate Richard and walk back with him.

From a window upstairs, Celia watched, hugging herself and deeply grateful that Richard was spending the time with his children.

Chapter Eight

The pond behind the inn was huge. It was a favorite attraction for the locals and tourists. During the winter, the inn would open it up to its guests and the public and have music and hot chocolate for the skaters as they enjoyed the beautiful ambiance. Cones were set up at the far edge to indicate where the ice was too thin and should be avoided.

Angela had convinced Sam to be their "D.J." for the afternoon. A small sound system was set up for music along with a microphone.

The weather was brisk and cool for the skaters as they came bundled up in their heavy coats, gloves, scarves, and hats. The storm was coming soon and everyone wanted a little outdoor time before that happened.

Christmas music softly played as Sam welcomed everyone to the pond. "Good afternoon, folks. Glad to have you here. Enjoy the skating and in a few minutes, we'll have different activities out on the ice so be listening for that."

The small children, when seeing him, couldn't keep from running to him and telling him what they wanted for Christmas. Sam would laugh heartily and listen to their requests. When the children saw Eldon brushing off the ice, they headed to him to ask what it was like to be one of Santa's elves. Eldon frowned and reiterated that he was simply short.

Everyone from the inn was there. Richard spotted Genevieve standing by the hot chocolate, watching him, smiling her feline smile. He smiled back and went over to talk to her. Celia found Lila to converse with. Huffing out sighs, the kids laced up their skates and headed for the pond.

The first game they played was "crack the whip." Several lines were formed, people holding hands and skating together. Invariably the last person on the chain would get waved back and forth. Bradley, to his mother's chagrin was at the end of one chain, hollering for all he was worth.

They had "adults only" skate and "kids only" skate. They had "women only" and "men only." "All skating" followed as Sam sought Bradley, Jenna, and Kevin. He gave each of them the finger by the nose signal, which they returned.

"All right everyone. Now it's time for a 'parent and child' skate. So, parents grab your child and hit the ice."

Jenna grabbed her dad, Kevin grabbed his mother. Bradley found his mother serving hot chocolate and said, "Come on mom. Let's go."

When she hesitated, Angela said, "Go on, Mary. I've got this covered."

Smiling, Mary laced up her skates, took Bradley's hand, and headed for the ice.

Sam found two children sitting out and took one over to Joe. "Joe, would you skate with little Liza here?" Before Joe could reject the idea Sam said, "She wants to skate and her mother is out there with her brother."

Looking down at the little girl, Joe grinned. "Sure." Taking her small hand, he led her onto the ice.

Sam took the other child to Dan. "Mr. Hamilton. Chris here needs a 'parent' to skate with since he came with a neighboring family. Would you be so kind as to skate with him?" And before Dan could say one way or the other, Sam added, "Thanks so much."

Looking down at the big-eyed little boy, Dan chuckled. "Okay, come on sport. Let's show them how it's done."

Sam walked over to Lila. "Miss Lila. I don't seem to have any of my children with me, so I was wondering if you might consider yourself my daughter for the duration of this song."

Lila put a hand to her heart. "Oh, Sam. I'd be honored." Allowing him to take her hand, they went to the pond. "You have children?"

He chuckled. "Oh, I have a whole bunch of them. They're back home with their mama while Eldon and I check out a few business ventures."

Grinning at the idea, Lila asked, "Is the 'Sleep in Heavenly Peace Inn' one of them?"

"No, we just like to stay here on our way through Vermont."

"Drat. You know, the owner of the inn seems to be a big mystery. Any chance you know who it is?"

"I have my guesses. Just like everyone else does. Angela is mute about the subject. Where's your home, Lila?"

"New York City. What about you?"

"Up north." Sam saw the questions in Lila's eyes. Before she could ask any of them, he looked around and said, "Nice crowd here today."

"Yes," she answered. "It's very nice of the inn to open it up to others like this."

"Yes, it's good to see the whole community out enjoying the Christmas season." They continued skating in silence. "Well, just look at that Mr. Hamilton." Sam noticed a slight interest come and go in Lila's eyes. "He seems to have gotten himself a little friend over there."

"Really?" Lila didn't even look.

"Yes." Sam laughed. "I think that little boy is having the time of his life with Mr. Hamilton."

She clearly didn't want to look. As Sam continued to laugh, she gave in and looked toward where he was pointing. Dan was skating with a young boy about six years old. Cute little boy. They were swinging their hands back and forth. At the high point of the swing, Dan would twirl the child around amidst his giggles. Lila smiled.

"That Mr. Hamilton is an interesting fellow. He's got a lot of talents, some not so clearly visible." Sam glanced at Lila.

She turned to gaze out over the assembly. "Yes, it is a nice crowd here today," she said putting an end to the conversation about Dan.

As the song came to an end, Angela got on the microphone. "All right, everyone. I know you've been waiting for this one. It's time for the couples' skate."

Bradley immediately pulled his mother over to Joe. "Hey, Joe, skate with my mom. She's too shy to ask you herself." Before either Joe or Mary could speak, Bradley took little Liza's hand and led her to the edge of the pond.

"Bradley," Mary said under her breath. She was horrified but instantly warmed as Joe smiled at her and took her hand.

"I've been wanting to skate with you all day," he said in that low, gravelly voice that made Mary's blood swirl. He took her in his arms and skated backwards leading her around the pond, both of them smiling.

Sam skated with Lila to where Dan was helping Chris off the ice. "Hey, Dan. Could you skate with Lila, here? I'm afraid my old bones are starting to stiffen up on me."

"Oh, no. That's all right. I'll just sit this one out," Lila said.

"Don't be silly. No reason to, when Dan would be happy to skate with you. Isn't that right, Dan?"

Looking at Lila's reluctant look and secretly enjoying her discomfort, Dan said, "Absolutely, Sam. Come on Lila." Before she could utter a protest, Dan had her hand and they were out on the ice.

They skated in silence for a while, Lila looking straight ahead, Dan lightly holding Lila's arm to guide her.

"That Sam is quite a character. I can't figure out who he really is or where he's from. Sorta like the owner of the inn," Dan said.

Lila's eyes went wide. "Right? I thought the same thing. He must be the most elusive person ever."

Grinning at her Dan said, "No. He's not the most elusive. You're avoiding me, aren't you?"

Lila was suddenly uncomfortable. "I'm not really avoiding you. It's just that we . . . well, we have nothing in common. There's really no reason for us to spend time together. Besides, you'll be leaving soon."

Dan's grin disappeared. He had been eager to get to Florida and it bothered him that he had forgotten that fact. "I guess you're right." He looked down into Lila's hazel eyes to see that they were like two pools of gold looking back at him. "My article is finished. I'll probably be leaving first thing in the morning."

She gave a little smile and said, "Have a nice trip, Dan."

He pulled her closer to him and said, "It's been nice seeing you again, Lila. I really mean it. I know I'm not your favorite person but . . . how about we have a nice skate together now before I go."

Lila smiled sincerely. "All right. Let's."

When the romantic ballad had started playing, Jenna saw Genevieve head toward her father. With big imploring brown eyes, Jenna looked up into her dad's face and said, "Daddy, would you please skate with me?"

Looking at his daughter's earnest face, he couldn't refuse. Smiling, he said, "Sure, honey."

Kevin had taken hold of his mother's arm strongly. "Come on Mom. Let's skate together some more."

She grinned at him. "You got it." They began skating together, doing spins and "figure eights."

Richard couldn't help watching and being impressed. They did "sit spins" and took turns skating backwards while holding hands.

He was itchy. "Hey, Jenna. Would it be all right if I skated with your mom?"

Acting as nonchalantly as she could, she said, "Sure, Dad."

They skated to where Kevin and Celia were spinning. When Celia saw Richard standing by, she nearly fell over trying to stop. "Hi," she said.

Smiling he said, "Hi." Not taking his eyes off Celia he said, "Kevin, how about you and Jenna skate the rest of the song. I want to see if your mother remembers our little routine."

"Oh, bring it on, big man," Celia said, fully up to the challenge. He took her in his arms and they skated away.

"No way am I skating with you," Kevin said.

Not offended, Jenna said, "Let's get off the ice and watch." As they stood on the side, they were impressed again with the athleticism of their parents. In college, Celia and Richard had taken first prize in the university's pair skating competition. The kids watched them mirror skate with ease. They jumped and did camel spins. When Richard lifted Celia in the air, he brought her slowly back down looking deep into her eyes. Jenna sighed loudly. Kevin looked at his sister and crossed his fingers. She repeated the action and they both returned their gaze to their parents, hoping that this might be the start of a new beginning for them.

After dinner, the wind outside began to pick up. Small flakes of snow were falling, and Joe kept glancing out the window as he helped Mary with the dishes.

"Are you worried about the weather?" she asked.

He nodded. "Something tells me this isn't just a small storm." Dropping the dishtowel on the counter, he headed for the door. "I'm going to check on the animals one more time."

Mary looked out the window. A chill went down her spine as she thought about what Joe said. Looking at the pegs by the door, she saw that

Joe's gloves had fallen out of the pocket of his coat. She wiped her hands and put on her own coat and gloves and took his out to the barn.

Standing at the door of the barn, Mary marveled anew at the gentleness Joe showed the animals. They loved and trusted him. So did she, she realized. She shook her head at the thought. It just could not be.

Not wanting to startle anyone, Mary whispered, "Joe?"

He turned and looked at her. "Mary, what are you doing out here. The weather's getting bad, you should be in the house."

She walked to him. "You dropped your gloves. I thought you might need them."

Joe took them and slipped them on. "Thank you," he said tenderly, the edges of his mouth lifted in a grin. The reindeer decided to let his presence be known at that moment with a grunt.

Mary and Joe walked over to him. As Joe patted him, Mary said, "How's the fellow doing?"

"Pretty well. I can't seem to find out who he belongs to or where he came from." Joe petted Dasher's nose as the animal lifted his head for the rub. "He seems to like it here."

Mary laughed. "Just what we need. A reindeer."

"I'm sure he'll get tired of being here and wander off. That is, if we can't find out who he belongs to.

Mary walked in front of the reindeer and smiled at him. Before she knew what had happened, Dasher's head bumped her making her fall into Joe. His arm came around her to settle her. "I like how this reindeer thinks," he said lazily. Mary was hypnotized, as she stared up into dark eyes.

Slowly as if in a dream, he turned her into his arms. He lowered his head to her as she lifted her arms around his neck. The kiss started gently but quickly turned into a firestorm. The desire they had for each other finally coming to a head, they both reached to be closer.

When he deepened the kiss, the sound of the wind disappeared, as all Mary could hear were stars exploding. All she thought was that it had been too long since she had felt this way. And she wanted. How glorious. Joe's rough hands began to softly come up her sides in tender touches, and all thought ceased in Mary's mind.

She was so sweet, sweeter than the most delicious honeycomb. Joe couldn't believe his good fortune to be alone with Mary, touching her, tasting her. His life had been so hard, filled with disappointment, terror, and violence. The softness of this kind woman was overwhelming. He would have liked nothing more, than to continue kissing her, showing her the depth of the feelings he had for her.

Keep your head, he told himself, making himself slow down. He wanted this to be the beginning of things for them, not just a "romp in the hay," pun intended.

Mary's body was taking over and her mind couldn't keep up with it. When Joe's lips moved to her neck, her throat, she tried to grasp that last line of reasoning. Slowly, she put her hands on his firm chest and slightly pushed. It was enough to have Joe looking up. "Mary?"

Breathless, she said, "Joe. This can't happen."

"Why not?"

"I . . . I have a son." Even she knew that excuse was feeble.

"I know. His name is Bradley. I happen to like him," Joe said dryly, as he rubbed Mary's shoulder. "That's not a good reason and you know it."

"It's more than that. Joe, I'm not a spring chicken. You should find a young woman that could . . . that could . . ."

Joe was totally confused. "That could what, Mary?"

"That could . . . you know, be a woman with you." Her face was heating up.

Shaking his head, he said slowly, "I don't know what that means. But I do know you're all the woman I want."

"No. No, it can't happen. It's not going to happen." And with that said, Mary quickly walked to the barn door. Looking back at Joe, trying not to let him see the tears in her eyes, she said, "I'm sorry, Joe." She raced back to the inn before her tears fell. Shutting the door behind her, her back against it, she closed her eyes and let the tears come.

She loved him.

She knew now how much she loved him, but she couldn't let him forsake the desires that a man had in order to be with her.

As she sobbed, a small voice drifted into her ears. "Mama?"

Looking down, Mary saw her small son, eyes looking up at her, concern in his face. She wanted to cry harder. Kneeling, she took him in her arms and held tight. "It's all right, honey. It's nothing. Mama'll be okay."

"Are you sure? I can ask Joe to fix something if it's broken."

Only my heart. "No, Bradley, Joe can't fix this. All I need is you and I'll be all right." She hugged him tighter. "All I ever need is you."

Back in the parlor, Richard was getting suspicious. He had been sitting on the couch talking to Genevieve when Jenna pulled him up to the game table for a round of "Apples to Apples." Kevin had been sitting there with Celia and Jenna told Richard that they needed him to be the fourth. "It's no fun with just three people," she had said.

Richard was just going to ask if Genevieve could join in, when Dan came in and finding Angela said, "Thanks for the advice, Angela. That hot tub after an afternoon of ice skating was just the thing." He added, "I feel great," before heading for the cookies and cider.

Rubbing his chin, Richard began to start putting things together. The laughter he heard from the kitchen when he and Genevieve had come back in from the lukewarm hot tub. The insistence from his kids that they spend every waking moment with him, excluding Genevieve. They even had him ice skating with Celia. It was all a plot.

And he was livid.

"Kids, Celia, I think we need to talk. Upstairs. Now." His voice was low and menacing. The kids looked at each other and paled.

In their suite, everyone took a seat, except for Richard, who paced back and forth. Before he lost his anger, he started on them. "You two think you're clever, don't you. Think you could pull the wool over your ol' dad's eyes. Well, I've got news for you. I'm on to you.

"I know you don't want your mom and me to get divorced. What kid does? But it's going to happen and I think it would be best for everyone if you just accepted it and moved on."

Tears started streaming down Jenna's eyes and Celia put her arms around her. "Richard. What's this all about?"

"They've been plotting, Celia. Haven't you noticed? They've been using all kinds of subtle ways to push us together. I can't believe you didn't . . . Wait a minute. You're not part of this, are you?"

"Part of a conspiracy to get you back? Please. The last thing I want is a husband who doesn't want me. I'm through trying to vie for your attention. You're free to go, as far as I'm concerned." Jenna cried harder. Kevin sat looking at the floor.

His anger eased and his heart constricted for his children. Clearing his throat, he bent in front of them. "Jenna, Kevin, you know that we love you. We'll never stop loving you or taking care of you. You know that, right?"

Sobbing, Jenna said, "We just wanted to have a nice vacation together."

"And we are." Richard sighed. "Maybe I was too hard on you. I just want you to play fair. We'll be together for a couple more days but no trying to push your mom and me together. Deal?"

Jenna and Kevin looked at each other. Slowly and without their parents' notice they slipped their hands behind their backs and crossed their fingers.

"Deal," they said simultaneously.

Lila came into the parlor and saw the cookies and cider out. She hesitated when she saw Dan standing there, but held her head up and walked over anyway. This was the new Lila, confident and self-assured.

Dan smiled when she approached. "Sugar cookies, my favorite," he said motioning to the platter of beige-colored cookies.

Taking a bite of one, Lila moaned her approval. "They're great." She poured herself a cup of cider and took a sip.

She really was lovely, Dan thought. Her light brown hair was shimmering down her shoulders in lovely waves. Her eyes, highlighted with a touch of makeup, were a deep brown reflecting the light from the fireplace. He would like so much to get to know her.

"So, are you all packed?" Lila asked.

"Yes. Joe's taking me to Burlington before breakfast in the morning." Before he could stop himself he said, "Listen, I'll be back in New York after the holidays. Could I maybe give you a call? We could have dinner if you like."

It was tempting. Lila would like to have dinner with Dan but she knew what would happen. She'd daydream a romance when that was the furthest thing from Dan's mind. She'd be devastated. All her hard work of becoming the woman she wanted to be would disappear and she'd have to start again.

She gave him a tentative smile and said, "Thank you for the offer, Dan, but I don't think so." She looked into the fire. "I . . . I have a lot going on right now."

He gave her a small grin. "Okay. But here's my card." He reached into his pocket and gave her a business card. "If you change your mind, or if you need anything, anything at all, don't hesitate to call me."

Lila looked at the card and nodded. She was proud of herself. She was being so adult. "I think I'll turn in now." Looking squarely at Dan she said, "Have a safe trip." Extending her hand to Dan she added, "Goodbye."'

"It's been a pleasure, Lila," Dan said in a tender voice that almost broke Lila's heart.

Before any more emotions bombarded her, she turned and headed to her room. She really was tired and needed sleep. She wanted to rest, to drift off into oblivion. Unfortunately, all her dreams that night would center on a tall, handsome man.

And what could have been.

Angela was straightening up the parlor as everyone had gone to his or her room when all of a sudden the front door blew open. In walked a large man, stocky and dark. He was in black from his wool hat covering his ebony hair to his black boots, sprinkled with snow. He quickly closed the door in the churning wind.

Angela stood and walked over to him. "Can I help you?"

"Yeah. I need a room."

"Well, I'm sorry but I'm afraid there's no room in the inn. Hey, that sounds familiar, doesn't it?" Angela chuckled.

However, the man was not amused. "Fine. I'll take anything you have—a couch, a cot, anything. There's nothing available in the whole town and it doesn't look like I'm getting out anytime soon."

Angela looked through the front windows and into the darkness. "What do you mean?"

Baffled, the man looked at her. "Lady, haven't you been listening to the news? It's coming. And it's not going to be pretty."

"Oh, you mean the storm. Well, we know all about that."

The man shook his head. "We're not talking about a winter storm here. We're talking fierce and violent. Bigger than anything in the past fifty years."

He looked into Angela's eyes and with distress said, "We're talking blizzard."

Chapter Nine

The wind howled and the snow blew all night long. While everyone was tucked safe and sound in their beds, the elements wrapped themselves around the little inn, testing the very fiber of the building. Utility lines were no match for the storm, causing Joe to crank up the generator in the middle of the night. Phone lines snapped like thin pieces of twine when accosted by the wind gusts. Snowdrifts hit the north side of the inn and barn, creating the sound of an encroaching army in the midst of a siege.

The storm raged on as morning broke and the guests began to wake. Coming into the dining room, Lila stumbled when she saw Dan sitting with a cup of coffee in front of him. Dan looked up and grinned at the surprised expression on her face. "No, he hasn't left yet," he said as if to answer the question in her eyes. "The roads and airports are closed until further notice."

"I'm sorry. I know you were anxious to get to Florida." To see some girl, Lila was sure.

"Nothing I can do about it right now, so." Dan lifted his coffee cup in salute. "Might as well enjoy it."

Richard, the kids, and Celia came in as Dan was explaining. "The roads are closed? For how long?"

"For at least the foreseeable future," Joe said as he brought in piping hot plates of freshly cooked pancakes. Celia and the kids made a beeline for the buffet.

"How long is that exactly?" Richard asked.

"Good morning, everyone." Angela walked into the room. "Have you heard the news? Looks like you all will be our guests for just a little while longer." She took a cup and added coffee.

"What do you mean? We're trapped here?" Richard was getting annoyed. "I've got plans. I'm supposed to be in St. Tropez the day after Christmas." Celia furiously cut into her pancakes.

"Oh, well Mr. Davis, I think you'd better call and cancel your plans." Angela thought a moment. "That is if your cell phone is getting reception. Our phones are out. They went out during the night."

Richard angrily picked up a cup and poured his coffee. Sitting next to Kevin, he pulled out his phone to search for a signal.

Bradley bounced out of the kitchen. "Hi Kevin, hi Jenna. Did you hear the news? We're having a balizzard!"

"A what?" Kevin asked.

"A balizzard. You know, when lots and lots of snow falls and covers a house so you can't even get out of the door and you're trapped inside for days and days!" Bradley's voice got more and more excited with each word.

"Cool!" Kevin said as he ate more pancakes.

"Daddy, does that mean we're staying here longer?" Jenna asked.

"There's got to be a way to leave if we want to go," Richard said. "This is ridiculous. It's not like we live in the 1800's."

"It's really bad," Sam said as he and Eldon walked into the room. They were covered in snow from head to toe. Sam turned to Joe. "Animals are all right. I gave them their breakfast, then attached a line from the barn door to the back door in case the wind gets so bad we can't see in front of us."

"Thanks Sam. As soon as there's a break in the storm, I'll shovel a trail to the barn."

"Those poor animals," Jenna said.

Sam smiled. "They'll be all right, sweetheart. God gave them nice, thick coats. And the barn is good and insulated from the wind."

"Wish we were," Genevieve said as she sauntered into the dining room. "I barely slept all night listening to that hideous noise." She poured herself a cup of coffee and sat next to Richard. "It was like sleeping next to a rock band."

Celia took a sip of coffee and whispered under her breath, "Which you've probably done." Jenna heard and giggled.

"Well, you'll love this next little piece of news," Dan said. "There's a blizzard. We're stuck here for a while."

Genevieve looked up from her coffee. "A while? How long's a while? I've got a photo shoot for Macy's next week. I've got to get back to the city." When no one assured her that they'd be gone before then, Genevieve lifted her big green eyes to Richard.

He didn't quite know what to say to the woman, while the rest of his family rolled their eyes at each other. "There's nothing any of us can do. I guess we just have to sit tight and wait to see what the weather does."

"I can tell you folks, it's going to be a while." Everyone turned at the unfamiliar voice. The kids looked up . . . and up to see the dark face of a stranger.

Angela quickly got up from her chair and hurried over to him. "Ladies and gentlemen, I'd like to introduce our newest guest. You could say he blew in with the weather last night." She chuckled at her joke. "This is Bo Shingle." Angela took his beefy arm in hers. "The poor dear had nowhere else to go so we made him a bed in the library." Graceful hostess that she was, Angela took Bo around the table to personally introduce him around.

Genevieve couldn't keep her eyes off him. As soon as he made it to her, she lifted her dainty hand high, expecting a kiss. Bo merely shook it and muttered a "hiya."

"Bo is a courier on his way to Montpelier. Isn't that interesting? So, if you have any questions on the delivery business, he's a good source," Angela said.

123

"I have a question, Bo. Can you deliver me to New York by the twenty-sixth?" Genevieve batted her long lashes at the man.

Not exactly knowing what to say to the woman, Bo replied, "Not in this weather, ma'am. Even my SUV four by four isn't going to make it through this weather."

"Oh, poo. I feel as if I'm stranded on a deserted island!" Genevieve said.

Kevin, Jenna, and Bradley looked at each other and giggled.

"Since we're all stranded together, let me go over some important information," Angela said. "First of all, do not go outside while it's storming. That is unless you help Joe with the animals in the barn. Even then, don't go out alone. Always go out in pairs. We'll have the NOAA radio on in the kitchen. You're welcome to go in at anytime to listen to the progress of the storm. I would strongly advise that you keep your cell phones charged. You have extra blankets in your rooms but if you need more don't hesitate to ask. That includes firewood. We've got plenty. Just ask Joe."

Then Angela added, "Oh, dear me, I almost forgot. I was going through my things last night and found these. I thought the children might enjoy them." From her front skirt pocket, Angela pulled out DVDs of *Gilligan's Island*. The children's eyes grew wide along with their smiles.

The others started talking, all commenting on how they could get through the blizzard. Angela just sat back and inwardly smiled. She had thought at first that the children would be the hard ones to keep entertained. Now she wasn't so sure.

Yes, sir, the plan was coming along nicely.

The next three days went by very slowly. The wind continued to howl and the snow continued to blow. And the guests of the little inn tried to find anything to keep them occupied. The men were constantly in the kitchen listening to the weather radio and drinking coffee. Twice a day Joe braved the elements to get to the barn and care for the animals. He always had a volunteer or two who just wanted to get out, even if it meant bracing himself for the short walk in the storm.

The women kept busy by baking, reading, chatting, or playing with the children.

The children were another matter altogether. The excitement of the blizzard had worn off after the first twenty-four hours and they were getting antsy. Celia and Richard took turns playing games with them. They had permission to build blanket forts in their suite and have quiet battles. Mary and Angela had them in the kitchen making Christmas goodies. Lila had story time with them each day, reading a favorite book to them. A small DVD player had been hooked up to the small television in the parlor cabinet. The children had watched so many episodes of *Gilligan's Island* they could quote the dialogue, and often did.

All in all, the inhabitants of the inn were doing okay—as long as the storm let up soon.

Lila walked to the music room to return sheet music she had borrowed. She loved going there. It was a cozy room with a baby grand piano tucked in one corner, a beautiful harp in another corner. Painted in soft, comforting hues of beige with mahogany trim, the room had an upholstered love seat along with a large display case with smaller instruments. A credenza held more sheet music than Lila had ever seen. She could have spent months going through it.

Before entering the room, Lila heard a voice from inside. Someone was making a personal call. Curiosity got the best of her when she realized the someone was Dan, and he sounded agitated. Lila leaned against the door to hear the conversation better, chiding herself for being so immature. She thought Dan was probably talking to his boss. Until she heard his words.

"I know, I know," Dan said into his phone. "I have no way of knowing when I can get out of here." He sighed heavily. "You know I'll get there as soon as I can." In a calm, loving tone he said, "I love you, Sarah," and clicked off.

I love you, Sarah. Lila felt her stomach drop. Of course Dan would have a girlfriend. That was why he was so eager to get to Florida for the holidays. What a ninny she was. She wanted to leave, to go back to her room and try to get Dan Hamilton out of her mind. Again. Quickly gathering her wits, she decided that she was going to square her shoulders, lift her head up high, just like she had done all those years ago. She was going to walk into that room and put the music away just like she had intended. After all, she was now confident. She was in control of her life. She was going to make her own path to the life she wanted—which didn't include Dan.

Carefully, she knocked on the door and opened it. "All right if I come in?" she asked lightly.

Dan was on the love seat wringing his hands, looking very nervous. The sight of him in that condition brought out all of Lila's maternal instincts and she wanted to go to him and comfort him. Instead, she headed for the music credenza as she softly asked, "Everything all right?"

Dan ran his fingers through his hair in obvious frustration and abruptly walked to the window where the snow still swirled against the wind. "I've just really got to get out of here. I think I'm going crazy. How much longer do you think we're going to be cooped up in this house?"

"I don't think it will be much longer."

Turning, Dan said, "Have you got a cigarette?"

"No. I didn't know you smoked."

Dan gave a short laugh. "I haven't for the past seven years. But it's either that or drink and I really don't want to start drinking at two o'clock in the afternoon."

Reaching into her pocket, Lila said, "Hey, I've got a stick of gum. Will that help?"

Dan gave Lila a smile and said, "Sure." He took the gum and popping it into his mouth began chewing avidly. Lila took a stick of gum and began chewing also. She finished putting the music in the credenza and turned to leave.

"Could you stay a minute, maybe sit and talk?" Dan asked as he sat back down on the love seat.

"Well, I really have to be going," Lila said feeling very warm in the small room alone with Dan. His large body took up most of the small couch and with the nervous energy radiating from him, he seemed dangerous.

A faint smile curved on his lips. "We're in the middle of a blizzard, darlin.' Where have you got to go?"

The endearment had her swaying toward the couch. It was like beautiful music to her ears. How pathetic, she thought. Even so, she walked to the love seat and sat down beside him. "I told Angela I'd help her make some cookies this afternoon."

Dan stretched his arm over the back of the little sofa. "Ah, yes, Angela. She's another one that's pretty mysterious, don't you think?"

"Maybe mysterious, but I think for the most part she's harmless." Lila smiled at the thought of the older lady. She had known only kindness and hospitality from Angela. However, Dan was right about the mysterious part. At times, she seemed a ditzy manager. At other times, she seemed very much in control, with a smile that held a multitude of secrets. Lila wasn't going to question it. She had enjoyed Angela's sunny disposition and optimism and would continue to while she was at the inn.

It was silent as Lila and Dan sat on the couch. Looking at Dan, Lila could see he was deep in thought.

He suddenly asked, "Have you ever thought about how fleeting life is? I mean, we think we have all the time in the world and then suddenly, we realize it's almost over. Just look at us. We're cooped up because of this storm, basically helpless to the elements, helpless to whatever life throws at us."

Lila had never known Dan to be so philosophical. She was confused. Gazing into his eyes, she saw many things. There was confusion, there was hurt, there was a wildness. If she hadn't been so fascinated, she would have run from the room. Instead, she sat there watching and listening.

"It just makes you think." Dan's fingers that lay on the back of the couch began caressing the ends of Lila's hair. His eyes took on a dark quality. "Time is so short, Lila. We never know what's going to happen today or tomorrow." With his free hand, Dan took his gum out and put it in the empty wrapper on the coffee table. Turning back to Lila, his hand that had been touching her hair went to her shoulders, kneading and rubbing. He moved over until he was sitting close to Lila. Extremely close. Lila could see the green of his eyes turn to deep emerald. "There are needs. So many needs yet to be filled."

Lila was mesmerized by the lull of his voice. As he leaned over, she thought, Great Scott, he's going to kiss me! Before she could decide what to do about it, his lips were on hers, rubbing and caressing. For a brief second, Lila was floating, in heaven, knowing what angels' singing sounded like.

But coming to herself, she backed away and slapped his face. Fury rose up in her instantly. How dare he think he can take advantage of their situation to put the moves on her. Apparently the gum, which incidentally she had swallowed, hadn't helped him relieve his tension so he wanted a woman. Not her, any woman would have sufficed.

Lila stood and stared at a puzzled Dan. Her voice low and threatening, she said, "Listen to me. I know you were the big man on campus in high school, having any girl you wanted. I know that now you're a big writer that goes all over the world. But you will never take advantage of me again, do you hear me?" She stomped to the door and before leaving said, "I'm sure if Genevieve isn't busy, she'd be happy to accommodate you. Or, you can wait until you get back to Sarah." She left, closing the door firmly behind her.

Dan sat in utter amazement. What a spitfire Lila had turned out to be. He had thought her sweet back in high school, had admired her brains. But now, she was enticing. And what was that about Sarah? He'd have to think about that one.

His mind went back to the problem at hand. He had to get out of this blizzard and make it to

Florida soon. Putting the gum back in his mouth he decided to use his energy on figuring out how to accomplish that.

Maybe it would take his mind off of the fact that he was starting to like Miss Lila Benson a little more than he should.

Chapter Ten

"I think the storm's finally letting up," Joe said to Mary as he shook off the snow from a trip outside.

"Good," Mary said as she stirred her hearty meat and vegetable soup. Since the scene in the barn, Mary and Joe hadn't said more than a dozen words to each other unless it had to do with the blizzard.

"Mary—"

"When do you think the electricity will come back on?" she interrupted, stirring vigorously.

Joe got the hint and stood back. "Don't know. The wind's down and the snow's slackened off. The power companies are probably working on it right now."

"So you think some of the guests can leave by tomorrow?"

Joe shook his head. "I don't see anyone leaving until sometime next week."

Mary turned to face him. "Next week!"

"Yeah. We've got about thirty-two inches of snow out there. It's going to take a while for the roads to be cleared all the way to Burlington and the airport to start running." Mary sighed. "We're just going to have to stick it out for a little longer. I think everyone's doing okay, considering."

"Maybe. But I'm about to run out of things for everyone to do, especially the kids. We've read every book, played every game, and we have enough cookies baked to last us the next two blizzards." Thinking hard she said, "Somehow I believe all the contained tension in kids and adults alike is going to break soon."

Joe chuckled. "Maybe I'd better open the lounge a little earlier tonight."

"That might be a good idea," Mary said and turned back to getting dinner ready. "I may be your first customer."

The tension was thick at dinner that night. Angela tried to lift spirits and keep the conversation going, but all she got for her troubles were mumbled responses and half-hearted smiles.

The kids were put to bed early that night, with prayers for a better day tomorrow. All the adults headed for the lounge. Joe was behind the bar, busy filling orders. After bringing in three plates overflowing with cookies, Angela settled at one of the small tables with Sam and Eldon, drinking hot apple cider, and speaking in soft tones.

Celia came up to the bar and smiled at Joe. "Could I have a martini, please Joe?" She brushed the strawberry blonde hair out of her eyes.

"Kids get to bed okay?" he asked as he made her drink.

She chuckled. "That's the hope, anyway. I left them with direct instructions to stay put unless it's an emergency." Joe put the drink in front of her as she took a sip. "I think they're getting as tired of me as I am of them." Then shocked for saying that, she looked up. "I really didn't mean that. It's just . . ."

Joe grinned. "No need to explain. Everyone's a little claustrophobic right now. We really need a break in this storm."

"It's not a whole lot different from the hurricanes they have in Florida when you think about it. Scotch rocks, Joe," Dan added as he sat next to Celia. "My parents live down there. I've been through a few storms with them, and after a few days you just want to get outside."

"Well, as soon as I can unearth my SUV, I'm out of here," Bo said sitting on the other side of Celia. "Give me a beer."

Celia turned to look at the man. He was big and hairy. Mysterious, even. Celia finished her drink and signaled for another. It had been a long time since she had sat next to a stranger in a bar. She wondered if she remembered how to flirt. "So, Bo. Tell me about yourself."

Bo took a big swig of his draft, wiping his mouth with the back of his hand. "What? Oh, well I'm originally from Rutland but now I own a courier service in Burlington. I was on my way to Montpelier to pick up some papers when the storm hit."

"Mmm. Fascinating." The alcohol was already beginning to relax Celia. "Tell me more. What's it like to be a courier?"

Bo was ready to plunge into his favorite topic—himself. As he launched into a discussion about how superior his business was to the competition, Richard came into the bar.

The first thing he saw was Celia sitting next to Bo, her eyes turned dreamily up to his. Richard didn't like it. He didn't like it one bit.

He took the stool next to Bo and slapped him on the back. "How's it going big guy?" Before Bo could answer his question, Richard turned to Joe. "How about a whiskey sour, Joe?" Richard watched Bo go back to talking to Celia. What was she finding so interesting in the guy? Richard couldn't help notice the way Celia's light hair caught the glow of the light. Her eyes were soft, dreamy. Just the way they looked after they used to . . . Richard didn't want to go there in his thinking. But she was the mother of his children. How many drinks had she had, anyway? Maybe he should step in and say something. As he opened his mouth to speak, Genevieve came waltzing into the lounge, wearing a long dress that clung to her body.

Celia thought she looked like she was going to an awards show. That is, an awards show about herself. Celia giggled at the thought as she finished her drink. "Joe? Another one of these please," she said.

Seeing Richard watching Celia, Genevieve rubbed her hand on Richard's shoulder and in a soft voice said, "Is this seat taken?" Sitting next to Richard she looked up at him and gave him her most powerful smile. Richard smiled back and tried to give his attention to the stunning redhead.

Mary and Lila walked in together and sat at a table. After a minute, Mary walked around to the bar to get two glasses of wine. Dan smiled at Mary and said, "I don't remember seeing you in here, Mary."

"I guess we're all at the point of needing a drink," she said without looking up.

"Well, good to see you in here. You give the place class." With that, Dan raised his glass in toasting Mary.

Looking up, Mary saw that he was serious. A smile broke across her face. And shamelessly, she winked at Dan as she walked back to the table with the wine.

Joe saw the exchange with glittering eyes. Scrubbing imaginary spills on the bar, he wondered how Dan would look with a black eye.

Down the bar, Bo had noticed Lila come in. He had always gone for petite brunettes. He left the bar and went to Lila and Mary's table.

When Bo moved, that left Celia staring directly at Richard and Genevieve. As a trained observer, Dan pretty much knew what was going on between the three people. He liked Celia. She seemed to be a good mother, a good person. She definitely was too good for the likes of Richard Davis. Dan leaned closer to Celia and they began talking in hushed tones.

Meanwhile, Bo was asking Lila all about herself. At first Lila was flattered. She started to tell Bo about her teaching and decided instead to talk about New York. Everyone loved to hear about New York. Sensing that three was a crowd, Mary moved to the barstool next to Dan. When Celia went to the restroom, Dan turned and started talking with her.

Joe thought maybe two black eyes would look better on the guy.

Hearing laughter come from behind him, Dan turned to see Lila giggling like a schoolgirl. He was incensed, for some reason. Excusing himself, he walked over to Lila's table. "Must be a good joke." Sitting down he said, "Mind sharing it?"

As Genevieve was ordering another drink, Richard looked down the bar. Mary was sitting there, looking miserable. Richard had been meaning to thank Mary for all her hard work and especially for keeping the kids occupied. He moved down the bar and sat next to her. "Mary, I can't thank you enough for all you've done during the blizzard."

"Well, you're very welcome, but I've just been doing my job." A giggle came from the other end of the bar. It looked like Joe and Genevieve were sharing a laugh. Mary's mood plummeted. If that wasn't enough, Lila hopped up to the bar to get another drink. When Joe handed it to her, she reached over and kissed him on the cheek. Was everyone running after Joe now?

Celia came back into the room at that time and sat in her barstool in front of Joe. Mary was

furious. She couldn't refrain from leaning over
and saying, "Well, Celia, aren't you going to have a
go at him?" When Mary tried to straighten, the pin
that she wore on her blouse got caught on
Richard's jacket. It locked the two of them tight
together, as if Richard was nuzzling Mary's neck.
"Oh, pardon me," she said, blushing profusely.

Joe headed down to that end of the bar
ready to do damage. He would have let Richard
have it if Bo hadn't stepped up to the bar and said,
"Hey, bartender. I don't much like your kissing my
girl."

My girl? Lila thought. He couldn't have just
said that.

"Yeah, well I don't take it too well when
someone's necking with *my* girl," Joe stormed.

About that time, Richard had gotten the pin
free and looked up to see Joe's violent eyes looking
at him.

"For goodness sake, Joe, my pin got stuck in
his jacket. And I am not your girl," Mary said
under her breath.

Richard turned to Bo, "And what are you
doing with Lila? I thought you were hitting on my
wife?"

"Richard!" Celia was embarrassed.

"Hey, guys. Let's just cool down," Dan said
coming to the bar and putting one hand on
Richard's shoulder and the other on Bo's shoulder.

"Shut up!" Joe, Richard, and Bo all said
simultaneously to Dan.

Richard said to Dan, "What's this to you?
First you're hitting on Lila. Then tonight you're at

Mary and Celia. What's the matter, buddy? Need a whole harem?"

"You're insane. I don't know what you're talking about."

"He's been hitting on my Lila?" Bo asked, rolling up the sleeves of his sweatshirt revealing monster biceps.

"Bo, what are you doing?" Lila was stunned.

"We're going to fight it out, honey. Just stay out of my way," Bo replied.

"This is ridiculous," Richard asserted.

"It's none of your business. Besides you looked like you were doing pretty well with the innkeeper!" Bo yelled.

Joe rounded the bar and faced Richard, "Yeah, what were you doing with the innkeeper, Davis? I'd really like to know?" He was toe-to-toe with Richard now itching to slug him.

"You want a fight?" Dan said to Bo. "You got it, Neanderthal!"

As fists were raised, Joe said, "Hey, wait!" All the men looked over. "Not in here. Mary will kill me."

Bo said, "Let's take it outside." Then thought better and said, "No, can't do that. There's a blizzard going on. How about arm wrestling for her?"

"I beg your pardon," Lila yelled, hands on her hips.

Dan answered, "No fair. Your biceps could crush Popeye.

Livid at the immaturity of the men, Celia said, "Well, you could always do what the kids do and play 'rock, paper, scissors.'"

"No, Celia. They probably wouldn't know what beats what," Lila sneered.

"I wouldn't mind a good fight," Genevieve said as she sat watching.

Celia had had it. She had just had it with that woman. She stepped over to her and said, "A good fight, is that what you want? Okay, lady, you've got it!" She reached on the bar and grabbed a handful of pretzels from a bowl and threw them at the stunned woman.

Quickly regaining her momentum, Genevieve took her glass and shoved it into the air causing the liquid to fly. Seeing this in time, Celia ducked and Richard got the gin and tonic straight in the face.

There was a slight pause in time as everyone contemplated the situation. Then it was a free-for-all, with everyone throwing drinks, pretzels, and bar nuts.

All this time, Angela, Sam, and Eldon had been watching, keeping their distance. When the first threat of a fight had been uttered, Sam started to stand but Angela's hand had restrained him. Now, as the eight "adults" continued throwing drinks and food at each other, she tried to hide a small smile. Sam saw it and he knew. Eldon continued to frown at the crazy people.

When it looked like the food was almost gone, Mary spotted the cookies on the counter behind the bar. She ran back and put two of the plates on the bar, holding back one for herself. Then they all started throwing cookies.

After throwing several cookies, Mary noticed that she felt marvelous. The tension was gone from her head and stomach.

She started to laugh.

And laugh and laugh. The others in turn started giggling, chuckling, until all of them were holding their sides from laughing so hard.

In between laugh spasms, Richard said, "I think we found the proper use for some of these cookies. I got hit with one that was harder than a rock."

Mirth in her eyes, Celia said, "That's because it was made by your son." More laughter.

Everyone was laughing so hard that they didn't hear Jenna at the back of the room call for her mother. Lila happened to look back and seeing the little girl, grabbed Celia and pointed to the back of the room. All eyes turned to see Jenna standing at the door, in her nightgown, holding a pillow.

Celia and Richard rushed to her. "What's the matter, sweetheart?" Celia asked.

"Mom, my tummy hurts. I think I ate too many cookies."

There was a brief moment of silence. And then everyone burst out laughing again.

A few minutes later, Bo hollered, "Everyone, hush!" They all stopped talking and laughing and listened.

"I don't hear anything," Genevieve said.

Dan smiled widely. "That's just it. It's quiet. The storm's over!"

Chapter Eleven

Everyone awoke the next morning, recharged after a night without winds howling outside the windows. The morning chatter was brisk, cheery, as everyone talked about going outside and breathing fresh air.

The previous night was laughed at while Kevin, Jenna, and Bradley looked confused. The bar had been a mess but thanks to a good hour of everyone working together before retiring last evening, it was completely cleaned, ready for another evening.

When Mary brought out hot platters of eggs and bacon, Celia said, "Mary, why don't you, Bradley, and Joe come sit with us."

"Oh, no. That's all right," Mary said, flattered but eager to be busy.

"No, Cee's right. Please join us," Richard said, and was echoed by everyone at the table.

Chairs were brought over and the three gratefully filled their plates and sat down. Bradley was practically bouncing up and down in his seat. "When can I go outside, Mama? When?"

"Son," she admonished. "We need to let Joe see what the conditions are like first. I don't want you walking outside and sink in snow over your head."

"Cool!" Kevin said.

"Hey Joe, I'll be glad to help you scope out the situation outside," Dan offered.

"Yeah, me too," Bo said between bites of eggs and toast.

"Count me in," Richard said. His children beamed at him. As did Celia.

Sam smiled. "Well, that's just fine. Eldon and I will help, of course. I think between all of us, we'll be able to make sure everything's safe around here."

"When do you think the airport will open up?" Genevieve asked.

Joe thought about it. "Not for a few more days, at least. Besides the airport, the highways need to be plowed. We just got the power back on this morning. Lots of places are still without. It's going to take some time."

"You mean I'm still stranded here?" she asked.

"Well, you may be, but I'm not. As soon as I've got my SUV dug out of the snow, I'm heading south."

Jenna looked at her mother. "Does that mean we're going to spend Christmas here?"

"It looks that way, sweetheart."

"Yay!" said Jenna as Kevin and Bradley added their approving hoots and applause.

Celia turned to Mary and Angela. "We really hate to put you out."

"Nonsense." Angela said. "There's nothing you can do about a blizzard. It's one of God's little inconveniences that make us stop and think. Besides, we love having you here." Looking at the others, she said, "We love having all of you here."

"Thank you, Angela," Lila said. "Mary, are there any more of those wonderful blueberry muffins in the kitchen?"

"Sure." Mary started to stand. "I'll get them right away."

"Sit, sit." Lila jumped up and hurried into the kitchen. "Does anyone need anything while I'm in there?" she asked.

Sam looked at Angela and she winked at him. The little group had become more of a family than they realized. She wished the good feelings would stay.

But sadly, they would not.

By lunchtime, the men were still working outside to shovel paths and remove snow from rooftops. The kids were so itchy to get outside they were bouncing off the walls.

Mary, Lila, Celia, and Angela sat at the kitchen table drinking cups of hot tea, watching the kids play on the floor with Bradley's cars and trucks. Angela's eyes sparkled as she watched the children play.

Seeing this, Lila asked, "Angela, do you have any children?"

She chuckled. "Oh, my no. But I've always had a special place in my heart for the little dears."

"Me too. But I sure would love for the little dears to be able to go outside and use up some of that never-ending energy," Celia said.

"Amen to that," Mary returned.

"I'm sure it won't be long now," Angela said. After taking a sip of her tea, she added, "You know, they'll still need to spend most of the time inside for the next few days." The mothers moaned and Lila chuckled. "But I was thinking, since you all will be with us for Christmas, why don't we have the kids put on a Christmas Eve program. Have it out in the barn with all the animals."

Jenna, having grown bored with playing cars, came over to her mom and put her arm around her. "A program? About Christmas?"

Warming to the idea, Lila said, "What a great idea. We could recreate the first Christmas and sing Christmas carols. It should be fun."

Hearing where the conversation was going, the boys got up and walked to the table. "I don't know. Have we gots the right animals?"

"Yeah, I don't remember a reindeer being in the stable at Bethlehem," Kevin added.

"I think the reindeer is a lovely addition. He could be Santa's contribution to the play, don't you think?" Angela asked.

Worried, Jenna looked at her mom. "Do you think Santa can find us here? We were supposed to be home for Christmas."

"I wouldn't worry, sweetheart. I'm sure that Santa knows you're here."

"Now, back to the program. Since we only have three children, I think we'll need the assistance of the grownups," Angela said. "Mary, how about you and Joe being a part of it?"

"Hey, Mary and Joe—Mary and Joseph. They can be Mary and Joseph!" Jenna said excitedly.

"Mama! You can be Mary and Joseph!" Bradley hopped around like a wild pogo stick.

Mary smiled at his enthusiasm. However, her stomach was not so sure about the idea. There were knots forming when she thought about playing the role of Joe's wife. Especially one that had just given birth. "Well, we'll see, honey. I don't know how Joe will feel about it."

"What about us, Miss Angela? What should we be?" Jenna said.

Smiling at the young girl, Angela said, "You, my darling, should be the angel that announces the birth of the Christ child." Turing to Bradley, she said, "And you, sweet Bradley, should be the shepherd out in the field who was first to hear the glorious news." Seeing Kevin waiting patiently, her smile broadened. "And you, young man, should be one of the wise men that looked for and found the newborn king."

Everyone in the kitchen was silent. The words Angela used held a calming sort of authority, so beautiful that it seemed almost sacrilegious to speak.

Angela took another sip of her tea and said, "Lila, dear, I think it would be a wonderful thing if you could lead us in singing."

"But how did you know . . ."

As Angela smiled, Mary said, "Don't fight it, Lila. Just accept that she knows."

Starting to get into the spirit of things, Celia said, "I can help with costumes and makeup."

As Jenna clapped her hands, Kevin moaned. "No way I'm going to wear that pretty girl stuff on my face!"

Celia chuckled and wrapped her arm around his neck, bringing his head over for a kiss. "All great actors wear makeup, including the actor you saw in the latest superhero movie. It'll help the audience see you. Oh, and it's pretty lady, not pretty girl."

"Well, if Captain America wore pretty lady, then I'm in," Bradley said. Everyone laughed.

"Oh, one more thing," Angela said, putting her cup down. Looking pointedly at the adults, one eyebrow raised, she continued. "I think perhaps we should give the lounge a rest tonight. Don't you think?" Three sets of guilty eyes returned her look. "Why don't we go into the music room tonight and have a good old-fashioned sing-a-long. Nothing better to get us into the Christmas spirit."

As everyone agreed, Mary couldn't help adding, "Yes, a great idea. I think we may even have some cookies left over to snack on." The room filled with moans and giggles.

Suddenly the back door opened and Richard came stomping into the kitchen. "Everything looks good. I was wondering if there were any kids here who'd like to explore a vast white wonderland?"

Deafening shouts and cheers filled the large kitchen.

After the men were plied with hot coffee and a hot lunch, everyone bundled up in their warmest gear to brave the still frigid weather. As Kevin, Jenna, and Bradley walked outside, they were immediately struck with the whiteness. Everywhere they saw was white. The snow had covered all the vehicles, all the vegetation, and all the outbuildings. There was a slight wind that chilled the bone quicker than the icy temperature.

Little Bradley's eyes were the only part of him visible to the elements and they were already starting to sting with the cold. Undaunted, he trudged ahead, wearing, he thought, every piece of clothing from his closet. Joe had instructed him to stay close, and as he saw the snow come up to his thigh, he decided that might be a good idea.

Kevin and Jenna were walking with their dad, each holding a hand. Jenna was sure that the North Pole couldn't look much different. They walked around the inn to the top of the little hill where the snow was the most shallow. "What are we doing here, Dad?" Jenna asked.

"I thought we might make a snowman on the hill. Maybe to guard the inn in case another blizzard decides to invade us." He smiled down at his children.

"Oh, yeah. Like a terminator snowman who will destroy the evil storms with his awesome power," Kevin said excitedly.

"Something like that," Richard said.

As she knelt in the snow and began scooping it up, Jenna said, "I think mine will be a handsome knight, determined to protect the princess in the castle inn."

Kevin pretended to gag as the three started their work. Joe and Bradley came walking up, glove-in-mitten, after them. "What you guys doing?" Bradley asked.

"We're building defenders of the inn. Want to help, Brad?" Kevin said.

With big eyes, Bradley looked up at Joe, whose heart melted as the love he felt for the child made him smile. He loved Bradley and wanted nothing more than to be his stepfather. Now, if he could only convince the mother. "Let's show 'em how it's done, Bradley."

Lila took a deep breath as she walked outside for the first time in days. The air was so cold, so clean it stung her lungs. The wind chaffed at her cheeks and made her eyes water.

It was wonderful.

She followed everyone around the inn, delighting in the beautiful pristine view of the land. Feeling like one of the first persons in a new land, she watched her footprints make deep marks in the fresh, white snow.

Everyone seemed to be heading for the top of the hill and there she saw the children busy making huge snowmen. She walked off to the side and fell back in the snow. After moving her arms and legs, she stood up to see her perfect snow angel.

The smile on her face was huge as Sam came to stand next to her. "Not bad, little girl. Now, let an old pro show you how it's done." And with that, Sam dropped back into the snow making his own large version of a snow angel. Lila giggled with delight.

She was beautiful. All bundled up and beaming—like the light from a Christmas tree. Dan just stood watching her. Her laugh floated through the air and as if having magical powers, rested deep within his soul. Rubbing his heart, Dan decided that this was crazy. Lila was right. She was better off without him. He was stuck here for another couple of days and then they would part. The idea didn't sit too well with him.

Well, if they were going to go their separate ways, what could be the harm in making snow angels together? None, he thought and headed for Lila and Sam.

The snow warriors were standing guard of the inn looking fierce and intimidating. Celia had joined her children in finishing the massive snowmen and sighed with exhaustion. "Whew!

What a big job." Hugging her kids closely to her body, she said, "Now I can sleep at night, knowing we're properly protected from anything outside."

Jenna smiled in satisfaction. "Mom, can we go make snow angels with Miss Lila and Sam?"

"Sure, honey. Go ahead." She watched as her kids ran over to fall back flat into the snow.

Celia laughed at them and noticing Richard standing nearby said, "They're going to be sopping wet by the time we get them back to the house." She looked at him and was puzzled by the strange expression on his face. "What's wrong?" she asked.

Slowly, he walked over to her. Moving a strand of hair away from her face and back into her cap, he said, "Nothing. Nothing at all." His face said different. His eyes were penetrating hers, his brows pulled together in a frown. Celia didn't know what to do, what to say."

"Richard?" came a light, feminine voice from behind them. They both turned and separated seeing Genevieve in her skin-tight jeans and her designer coat walking toward them. She approached Richard and slid her arm around his. "I thought maybe you could walk me around the grounds. Show me everything. I'm a little frightened to go by myself." She brushed at his jacket to clear away a stray snowflake.

"Of course." Nodding to Celia, he and Genevieve left for their walk.

Celia was left alone, feeling a deep, deep hole in her heart. She sighed heavily and walked over to view her children joyfully playing in the snow.

That evening after supper, everyone wandered into the music room for dessert—not cookies, but fresh gingerbread with homemade whipped topping. As everyone enjoyed his or her dessert with coffee or milk, Lila sat at the piano. She began to softly play Christmas pieces that she had memorized over the years. Dan racked his brain trying to remember if he had ever heard her play. Obviously she had studied as a child and was very proficient at it.

The little group quieted down as she began to softly sing "The Christmas Waltz." Everyone was spellbound. Her soft and richly vibrant voice rang through the room. Even the kids had stopped eating to watch the lovely young woman sing about the wonders of the Christmas season.

When Lila finished the song she looked up to the smiles and thunderous applause from her new friends. A kind of joy spread through her that she had never had before. She felt loved, appreciated, accepted. Tears threatened to fill her eyes and pushing them back she said, "All right, everyone. It's your turn, now."

They began singing Christmas songs, everything from "Away in a Manger to "We Wish You a Merry Christmas." They divided up into groups and sang "The Twelve Days of Christmas" laughing so hard, the words were difficult to get out at times.

Before everyone knew it, it was eleven o'clock. Mary hurried Bradley along after Angela assured her that she would straighten up the music room. Joe watched them leave with longing in his eyes.

Richard's eyes met Genevieve's but before he could approach her, Jenna tugged at his hand. "Please, Daddy. Could you read me a story before bed?"

"Sure, Princess," he said, leaving with Jenna, Kevin, and Celia.

Dan walked over to Lila as she gathered up the Christmas music she had found in the room. "Very impressive," he said as he hit a few piano keys. "I didn't remember you playing."

With no emotion in her voice, Lila said, "Not surprising. You didn't know very much about me."

Before he realized what he was saying, he whispered, "Maybe I'd like to."

Lila closed the cover to the piano, threatening to snag his fingers. "I wouldn't."

Finally, only Angela, Sam, and Eldon were left in the room. They each took a seat and stretched their legs.

"I don't know, Angela. Doesn't seem like anything's moving along. I thought maybe with that blizzard and our being shut up together things would happen," Sam said.

Angela rubbed her cold arms. "Don't be fooled. There's a lot going on, a lot of hurt that needs to be worked through. Secrets that need to be told."

"But the roads will be cleared in less than a week." Sam sighed. "I hate to say it, but I think I'm losing faith here."

Angela patted his hand. "I understand, Sam. But trust me, it's not over. All they need is a little time together, uninterrupted. That's what the owner says." Looking straight ahead, she said, "Things are going to heat up. Starting tomorrow, as a matter of fact."

Sam and Eldon looked at each other, then back at Angela. "What should we do?" Sam asked.

Angela thought. "Be observant. Be ready with patience. Be ready to help and most importantly, be ready to comfort." With affection, she smiled at the two and added, "Just like I taught you."

Chapter Twelve

Early the next morning, Mary was in the barn gathering eggs for breakfast omelets. She was enjoying the quiet of the morning, when Joe came in. Her heart gave a quick flutter and banking down the obvious attraction she felt for him, she said, "Good morning."

"Morning. Angela said you'd be out here. She wanted me to tell you she needs eggs."

Smiling, knowing that Angela had planned their meeting, Mary said, "Of course she does."

"Could I give you a hand?" Joe asked tentatively and without waiting for her assent he walked over to help her gather eggs. "You know, we really haven't had any time to talk in the past several days."

Mary had thought the same thing. She missed those times. She and Joe were so alike in their values, in their interests, in most things. "Well, it's been pretty busy around here."

Joe chuckled. "I guess I owe you an apology for what happened in the lounge the other night. We all got a little crazy."

Mary giggled. "I'll never forget the expression on little Jenna's face when she walked into the room. It was like she was the adult and we were the children." They both laughed.

"You can't blame me for making a fuss, Mary. It really did look like you and Davis were snuggling with each other." Just the thought of that made Joe's blood boil.

Continuing to gather eggs, Mary said, "I'm sure it did. But you know that I have no feelings other than friendship for any of our guests."

Joe took the basket from her and set it down. Turning her to face him, he said, "What about the handyman, Mary. Do you have any feelings for him?"

She looked up into the dark, serious eyes she had grown to love. She had to be honest with him. "Yes, Joe, I do."

Joe wrapped his arms around her and for a moment, just reveled in the feel of her. As Mary stretched her arms up his back, Joe lowered his mouth to her neck and softly kissed her. The sweetness he found made his breath clog in his throat. This was what he wanted in his life. This was all he ever wanted. He continued to spread little kisses on her neck, her ear, her cheek. Mary moved her face and their lips met in the fiery passion that was becoming addictive. Joe would never have believed that such fervor could exist in his sweet Mary. It entranced him, made him want her with a desire so hot that it threatened to burn his clothes.

They kissed until they were both breathless. Joe whispered, "I love you, Mary."

"Please don't say that, Joe."

"Why not? I don't want to try and hide it anymore. I want to make a life with you—you and Bradley. I want to be your husband, your companion, your lover."

As Joe held Mary's shoulders, she shook her head. "No. It won't work."

"Why?" Joe asked with frustration.

"It just wouldn't." She turned her head as tears filled her eyes.

"Mary, you've got to tell me why we can't be together." When she didn't speak he said, "It's Patrick, isn't it. You can't see yourself with anyone but him."

Mary looked back at Joe. "No, it's not. Patrick was a wonderful husband, a wonderful father. But I know that he's gone and that he wants me to go on with my life."

"You're right about that." Joe rubbed Mary's shoulders. "We did a lot of talking in Afghanistan. We talked about everything, our lives, our dreams, our hopes. He talked about you all the time and he showed me Bradley's picture at least ten times a day. He thought the sun rose and set with the two of you."

Mary let the tears fall, remembering all that she had lost.

"When you're in situations like we were, you talk about things. 'What if' things. Patrick made me promise that if something happened to him, I'd take care of you two."

The tears stopped and Mary narrowed her eyes. "He made you promise what?"

Confused, Joe said, "He made me promise to take care of the both of you if something happened to him."

Mary's eyes began to blur, not with tears but with rage. "That's why you came here? To take care of us? That's why you want to be with me? Because you're honoring a promise you made to my late husband?"

Joe was in trouble. He knew he was in trouble but wasn't quite sure why. "What's wrong with that?" he said in his defense.

Mary backed away from him. "What's wrong with that?" She tried to calm herself by stopping and balling her hands into fists at her sides. "Joe, I know you. You're an honorable man." Her heart hardened with a new realization. "You don't love me, you're just trying to keep a promise that you made to your friend, that's all. But I'm not going to let you throw your life away because of some promise. You've seen us and we're doing fine. Consider your promise kept."

"Throw away my life?" Now just as angry as Mary, he walked to her. "Didn't you hear what I said, woman? I love you. That wasn't part of the promise. And, by the way, it was never intended or expected on my part. The falling in love with you and Bradley just happened."

"Well, you better make it un-happen because nothing's going to happen!" Mary was so livid she wasn't making any sense. "How dare you want to marry me out of duty. It's insulting."

Getting in his face, she cried, "And for your information we don't need your pity. Go find another charity case!"

"Stop yelling at him!" Bradley was standing at the barn door holding Sam's hand.

"Bradley, what are you doing here?" Mary asked, instantly repentant for her explosion.

When Bradley didn't say anything, Sam said, "We just came in to give Dasher his breakfast." Bradley stood glaring at his mother.

"Honey, Joe and I were just . . . having a discussion."

"You don't want him. You don't want me to have a dad. I hate you!" Bradley said before he ran back to the inn.

"Bradley!" Mary ran after him.

Joe started toward the inn, but Sam's hand stopped him. "They probably need a little time alone right now."

"Yeah, I guess you're right," Joe said reluctantly. "How about giving me a hand with breakfast," he said as he made his way to the animals.

"Glad to." He stopped to pet the reindeer's back while he studied Joe. The man was hurting. Sam's heart went out to him. "You know, sometimes there's more to a person than meets the eye."

"How do you mean?" Joe asked as he took two buckets and filled them with grain.

"I have a feeling that Mary's not telling you the whole story."

"What is wrong with her?" Joe angrily said. Sighing he said, "I'm sorry, Sam. I just don't understand that woman. We could have everything together and she wants to fight me on it."

"Everything?" Sam asked.

"Everything I've ever wanted, anyway. Maybe it was just a selfish dream on my part, the idea that the three of us could be a family."

"Not selfish. A beautiful, completely natural dream, as I see it."

"Well, apparently, it's not going to happen. Help me with this water, will you?"

"Sure." Sam followed Joe. "One thing I've learned about dreams, though, is that you can't give up. No matter how hard it gets."

"Listen, the lady said no. How many times do I have to hear it before I know she means it? Why would I put myself through that rejection over and over?"

Uneasy, Sam asked, "What are you going to do?"

"I'm giving my notice. I'll stay until the first of February."

After breakfast, Joe was back in the barn, finding busy work to keep him away from Mary. He just couldn't be near her. He was liable to yell in her face. Or beg at her feet. Neither option seemed appropriate.

"Is the coast clear, Joe?" Richard asked from the door.

"If you mean is the barn empty of children, then yeah. The coast is clear." Still in a rotten mood, Joe got a pitchfork and began cleaning out the stalls, pitching the old hay into a wheelbarrow.

"Great." Richard walked in and rubbing his gloved hands for warmth walked over to Joe. "I just wanted to check on the presents. Do you mind?" Before leaving New Rochelle, Richard had shipped several of Jenna and Kevin's Christmas presents to the inn. His thought had been that it would be fun for them to open a few gifts while on their "family vacation." Now he thanked his lucky stars that he had done that, since they would be at the inn on Christmas Day.

"Knock yourself out," Joe said as he continued to work.

Richard walked over to the back corner of the barn where the presents lay under a huge tarp. He looked them over and satisfied that everything looked okay, replaced the tarp and started to go. The anguish that he saw on Joe's face stopped him. Usually Joe had a very serious expression, one devoid of emotions. Richard had come to trust the handyman on matters of living through a blizzard. He was certainly glad that Joe had been with them through the whole ordeal. It seemed strange to see the man filled with pain.

Stopping by the rail of one of the stalls, Richard leaned over it and said, "Something bothering you, Joe?"

The question obviously took Joe by surprise. "Yeah, something's bothering me." Joe stood up and leaning on the pitchfork, studied Richard. "I can't understand a man like you."

Confused, Richard said, "I beg your pardon?"

"Look at you. You've got a beautiful wife and two great kids. And you're throwing it all away. I just don't get it."

Richard tensed all over. "No offense, but it's really none of your business."

"I know. You're right. But there's no law against making observations and buddy all I see is that you're breaking the hearts of your sweet family. All because *you* want to leave. In my book, that doesn't make you the brightest bulb in the bunch." Joe went back to work.

Richard stood there stunned. Joe wasn't much of a talker. That was the most he'd heard him say at one time. But he was wrong. The marriage was over. He felt the most humane thing to do was leave before more damage was done. Richard respected Joe and wanted him to see that. "It's not like I wanted a divorce. We were arguing all the time, the kids were starting to suffer for it. What am I suppose to do? Stay in the relationship and pay for their therapy sessions?"

"You're supposed to stay in the relationship and work it out! Man, I can't believe an intelligent man like you is so dumb. Your kids adore you. They don't want to lose you. And that wife of yours? Anyone with eyes can see that she's still in love with you. Man, do you know what I would give for a life like that? Everything, buddy. Everything."

They were silent for a moment, each involved in their own thoughts. Finally Joe shook his head. "I've said enough. If Mary hears about this, she'll . . ." What did it matter if Mary heard about it? He was leaving anyway. "Look, you're accountable for your own actions. You'll reap the consequences, believe me." Going back to his own reserved self, he added, "Whatever."

What could Richard say? After an awkward silence, he said, "Yeah. Whatever." He walked out of the barn and decided to go for a short walk. Joe thought that Celia was still in love with him. It couldn't be. They had agreed—a divorce was the best thing. He had made plans, other plans that didn't include her.

Of course the plans didn't include his children, either. What kind of father was he? He was a good father. Hadn't he even agreed to this stupid vacation because they wanted one last family vacation together?

He hated the idea of hurting them. He hated the idea of hurting Celia, for that matter. No matter how he felt about her, she still had been a good wife, a good mother to his children. He'd make sure that she was taken care of.

Still, there had been moments on this trip when he'd felt something for her. He remembered her eyes when she was skiing or skating, how alive and vibrant they were. He enjoyed the subtle scent that she wore that was light, airy, delicious. He loved watching her with the kids, so full of compassion and love. He would miss all those things about her.

But they'd agreed. They had simply changed. It was time to move on. *Get a grip, Davis.* The sooner this vacation was over, the better.

Lila had always loved animals. In Iowa as a girl, she always had pets. Farms were within driving distance, where she could get her fill of horses, cows, and chickens.

After getting the okay from Joe who seemed to be in a surly mood, Lila walked into the barn to visit all the animals. As she lingered to pet each one, she thought about how simple their lives must be. No problems with confidence. No problems with romance. She sighed. Would she ever find the right man? Yes, she determined, she would. But she had to be happy with herself first.

Lila smiled. She was. She was learning how to make herself pretty, how to assert herself. Being comfortable in her own skin was a new experience, a scary one at times but she was getting there.

Stopping by the sheep, she sat down to hug them. Their coats of wool felt soft against her cheek. She enjoyed listening to their soft "Baa's."

While Lila was enjoying the moment, she heard heavy footsteps along with whistling. She stood and looked over the rail to see Bo looking through some boxes on a shelf against the wall. The sheep started protesting Lila's lack of attention loudly, causing Bo to turn and look. A huge smile covered his face. "Hey, there Lila. I didn't see you." He dropped the box and turned to give her his full attention. "But it sure is a nice surprise."

Lila wasn't pleased about being alone in the barn with Bo. She straightened up and said, "What are you looking for?"

"Oh. Joe said there would be an extra set of chains in here. My SUV needs more."

"Are you leaving?" Lila was hopeful.

Bo chuckled. "Just as soon as I can." He leaned back and crossed his arms, giving Lila a head-to-toe scrutiny. "You play your cards right, little lady, and I'll give you a ride. Anywhere you want to go."

Lila wiped the hay off her jean-clad legs and walked out of the stall, edging toward the door of the barn. "No thanks, I'm scheduled to be here another few days. Besides, I wouldn't want to hold you up."

Bo walked closer to Lila, blocking off her access to the door. "I bet I could make you change your mind, baby doll."

She was not going to sweat. Never let them see you sweat. "Bo, I want you to move so I can leave, please," Lila said in a calm voice, the nerves below the surface.

Dan approached the barn door looking for Lila. The kids had asked him to find her so they could practice the music for the Christmas Eve program. He heard voices and stopped to listen.

"Yes, sir, you are a real piece of work. Just the kind I'd like to know better. Come on, I know you want a piece of the Bo-ster." He flexed his enormous bicep. "No woman can get enough of this. Don't play hard to get, Lila."

"Bo, I'm warning you to leave me alone." Dan was in the barn in a flash—just in time to see Lila twist that enormous bicep back and knock the backs of Bo's legs out from under him. Bo lay on the ground looking up at the ceiling, his large eyes unfocused.

Dan came rushing to Lila. He took both her arms and looked into her dazed eyes as he felt her tremble. "Lila, are you okay?"

"Yes," she whispered.

"What happened?" Dan said, turning to look at the massive human laying on the ground.

"Bo was . . . coming on to me . . . I didn't want to . . ." Lila was trying very hard to draw in a full breath. "It all happened so fast."

Trying to get up now, Bo looked in admiration at Lila. "Wow. That was some kind of move, little lady. I'm impressed."

Dan put a protective arm around Lila's shoulder. Okay, it was too little too late, but he figured that he was there now. He'd protect Lila. "Don't you come near her."

Bo looked at Lila, his expression apologetic. "I thought you were interested. You seemed that way the night at the lounge. But I get the message now." He rubbed his bruised bottom and brushed hay out of his hair. "You're amazing, Lila. If you ever change your mind, give me a call." Leaving with his damaged derrière and cracked ego, he chuckled under his breath. "Never saw it coming."

They watched him go. Lila suddenly realized that Dan's arm was still around her. She quickly stepped away. "Well, I'd better go," she mumbled, losing all the bravado she had had with Bo.

"Yeah, the kids need you in the music room to go over some songs."

She smiled. "Fine."

"Lila." She turned back at the calling of her name. "That really was impressive. You're an incredible woman."

"Thank you," she said sincerely, and left the barn.

What was she doing to him? Dan had never been so consumed by a woman before. He couldn't get her out of his head. He'd argued with himself so many times in the last week about Lila. Could it work? Of course it couldn't work. Did he want it to work? Yes. No. He was dizzy trying to work it through his mind. But he always came back to the bottom line.

She didn't want him.

She had made that abundantly clear.

As Dan sat mindlessly watching one of the *Gilligan's Island* reruns, he thought how ironic the situation was. Years ago, he had been the one to walk away. Now it was Lila's turn. Wouldn't his old friend Russell have a field day with this?

Russell. Just thinking of the man brought an ache to his heart. He had to get out of Vermont and soon, before it was too late.

168

"Deep thoughts, young man?"

Dan looked up to see Sam standing by him. Grinning, Dan said, "Deeper than the snow, Sam. Why don't you pull up a chair? We can see if the seven stranded castaways get off the island."

Chuckling Sam said, "I have it on good authority that they don't. At least not in these DVDs." He looked at Dan's hard face. "I was just thinking of going for a walk. Maybe you'd like to join me."

"I don't know. Walking in this mess might be pretty hard."

"Then let's put on snowshoes." Sam saw Dan's hesitation. "Now, you're not afraid of an old man showing you up on the things, are you?"

Dan's face split in a grin. "You old? Never. All right, Sam, you win. Let's go for that walk." Dan stood, slapping Sam's back and heading for the back door.

Yes, a long walk and a good talk. That's what Daniel Hamilton needs right now, Sam thought.

Bradley had been in his room all day. Mary had tried to talk to him but he had completely shut her out. She had left the little two-bedroom apartment on the third floor that they occupied to give him time to cool down.

Working in the kitchen, her mind kept racing back to her little boy, the heartbreaking expression on his face before he had run from the barn. She thought about Joe and her feelings for him. It was all such a mess. Her mind was so distracted that she nearly cut her fingers several times as she cut vegetables for the "Santa Stew" that she was making.

She heard a noise on the back staircase and turned to see her little son, his eyes red from crying, holding his Pooh Bear. His father had given the plush animal to Bradley when he was born and whenever Bradley was scared or angry or depressed, he carried Pooh Bear with him.

Emotion clogged Mary's heart as she struggled with the right words to say. Not knowing how to help him, she settled with the old mother's standby, "Are you hungry, honey?"

He shook his head and walked over to the counter where his mother was working. He climbed up and sat there holding Pooh, looking out the window. Slowly, Mary went back to her vegetables, waiting.

After five long minutes of silence, Bradley said, "What was my dad like?"

Of all the things Bradley could have said, Mary never would have guessed that would be one of them. Tears filled her eyes as she looked at her precious child.

She put down her knife, washed and dried her hands. Leaning against the counter, she smiled and said, "You look just like him."

"Really?" Bradley said with big eyes.

"Yes." Mary took a breath. "Your dad was the smartest, bravest, most wonderful man I knew. He not only had a kind heart, but he had a courageous spirit that made him want to make the world a better place." She tentatively stroked his hair and continued. "A better place for his son to live in."

"Why did he have to die?"

Mary had known that question would come up one day. Bradley had been too little at the time of Patrick's death to question it. She hadn't been ready to give him an answer. She felt no more ready at this moment. "I don't know, honey. I can't give you an answer unless it's that I guess it was his time to go. But I do know that he's in heaven watching over us."

"He is?"

"Yes. And I know that he's very proud of his boy."

Footsteps behind them caused them both to turn. Joe came through the kitchen, stopping only to place an envelope by the kitchen sink, not looking at Mary or Bradley. He continued to the mudroom where he put his winter gear on and went outside. It was quiet after the door closed.

"Is Joe smart and brave and all those other things that Daddy was?"

Mary rubbed Bradley's shoulder. "Yes, he is, sweetheart. All those things."

"Then why—"

Mary put her fingers over his lips to stop the question. "Bradley, some things just cannot happen. When you're older you'll understand what I mean." Taking a breath, Mary said, "Now, we need to put this morning behind us, all right?" She turned back to the sink and her vegetables.

"I've got to get this stew going. How about you straighten up the living room of our apartment?"

Resigned, Bradley hopped down from the counter and headed for the stairs. Turning, he said, "Mom? When I grow up I'm going to be just like Daddy . . . and Joe."

Tears stung her eyes. "I think that's a good plan."

When Bradley left the room and she was sure that she was alone, Mary dried her hands and opened the envelope Joe had left. Her heart stopped when she read the words. "Letter of resignation."

Chapter Thirteen

"I could teach you how to ski downhill,"
Dan said to Lila as they enjoyed an after dinner
cup of hot chocolate. Dan's walk that afternoon
with Sam had been invigorating in many ways. He
was still amazed he had opened up to the man he
had known for such a short time. Sam had listened
patiently, sharing bits of wisdom from his long life.
There was just something about the older man.
After their walk, Dan was encouraged and,
strangely, at peace. Finding Lila in the parlor had
been a side benefit, one that he wasn't going to let
slip away.

"There's a small hill next to the inn. How
about we get some skis on in the morning and I'll
show you how to make it down."

"I don't know, Dan. You remember what I
looked like the last time I attempted to ski." Lila
was mortified that Dan had seen all the snow
packed on her snowsuit, the result of so many falls.

"Maybe you didn't have the right teacher,"
Dan said casually. "I could get you going down the
hill like a pro. No problem."

"It's tempting."

"Come on, give it a chance."

She really did want to know how to ski. Besides, Dan seemed different. He seemed more at ease, less fragmented. Maybe he had spoken to his beloved Sarah and was in a good mood. Perhaps they could spend a morning together without anything bad happening.

Which was why she was on top of the little hill the next morning, poles in gloved hands, standing in a crouched position. She felt ridiculous. However, she listened carefully to Dan's gentle instructions. The first time down, she fell two times but Dan was right there to help her back up and encourage her along. At the bottom, they took off their skis and trudged back up to try again. This time, Dan skied backwards in front of her, guiding her as they made their way down. Lila tried to concentrate on her skiing instead of the incredibly handsome and athletic man in front of her. He glided down without any problem and Lila loved watching him. All of a sudden, she realized that she was at the bottom of the hill, having made it without a tumble. She was so excited that she squealed loud and long. Grabbing Dan, she hugged him tightly saying, "Thank you. Thank you."

"Your welcome," he said softly in her ear. Pulling back from her, he added, "But you're not finished. Let's go again."

An hour later Lila was cruising down the hill, no problem, hooting and hollering, having a ball, Dan laughing with her.

"Let's take a final run and go get some coffee," he said.

Their last run down started out nice and easy. Lila was cutting back and forth just like Dan had instructed her to do. She went about halfway down, and cutting back across, stopped. Dan was coming behind her and couldn't stop before bumping into her. When their bodies collided there was a brief second of stillness and the two fell over as one unit, both laughing aloud. Their angle was so awkward as they tried to stand with their skis, they both fell back in the snow.

To help the situation, Dan took off his skis, his eyes on Lila. She was a vision. Her cheeks were glowing and her eyes were full of fun. She had snow caked on the sides of her hat framing her face like a snow angel. Knowing how cold that must be, Dan reached over and brushed off the snow, watching her eyes shine. He could have very easily taken her in his arms and kissed her. But he reminded himself that she didn't want that. And he shouldn't want that. He had to keep his priorities in mind.

He helped her up and they took their equipment back to the shed, Lila chattering happily all the way.

She was so proud of herself for sticking with it and learning the sport. Closing up the shed, they saw Eldon heading to the barn with a bucket of grain.

Lila stopped him. "Eldon, what's that you've got?"

With the permanent frown on his face, he said, "It's a special recipe of grains for the reindeer. Thought I'd take it to him now."

"Oh, let me, please."

Shrugging, he handed the bucket to her and headed back to the inn.

"Come on," Lila said taking Dan's hand. "Let's feed Dasher."

Inside the barn, they walked over to Dasher. "How you doing, boy? We've brought you a snack." Lila walked into the stall and put the bucket in front of the reindeer. As Dasher began eating, Lila took off her gloves and patted his back, delighting in the feel of the animal's tender hide.

"Did you have any animals in Iowa?" Dan asked.

"Not really. We lived in town so the best I could do was a dog and a cat. One time we had a canary. Oh, and one Easter I got a rabbit, but that's all. How about you?"

"We had a few horses and chickens out at our place. The chickens, of course for the eggs, and the horses for fun. My buddies and I used to love to go riding."

"I loved to ride. My parents were friends with old man Bevins. He used to let me ride one of his horses. I think it was the best thing about Iowa."

"You ever ride in Central Park?" Dan asked.

She shook her head. "No. I never seem to have the time." Feeling his eyes on her, she glanced up at him. "What is it?"

176

"Your eyes are green now. Fascinating." He leaned over the rails of the stall and continued to stare. "It's a pleasure to watch you, Lila."

She laughed. "You're not giving me another line, are you?"

"No. I'm not giving you any more lines. After all, I don't want to end up like poor Bo."

"Well, it served him right," she said, giggling. After a hesitation, she said, "I can't imagine me doing the same thing to you, though."

"Why not?"

What should she say? Because she didn't know if she would want to stop him? "Uh, because . . . I've lost the element of surprise with you." Did that sound believable?

Dan smiled and walked into the stall to pet the reindeer. He stood close to her as he said, "Don't worry, I know when to stop pursuing."

"Pity." The word was out of her mouth before she could contain it. Dan looked at her with a surprised grin. "I mean . . . it's just . . . that . . ." She was stuttering. She hated to stutter.

She admitted to herself that she wanted him to make a move on her. She wanted to feel his arms around her, his lips on hers. She was tired of playing the victim. She wanted to take complete control back over her life. Right now, there only seemed one way to do that.

"Oh, what the heck." She grabbed Dan by the lapels of his coat and pulled him to her. Her mouth closed firm over his as her heart drummed in her chest. Even if he pushed her away, laughed at her, at least she had shown the confidence to take the first step. She would be proud of herself.

Later. After she stopped feeling his lips move over hers and she could think. His arms came around her, pulling her close. She felt herself melting in the cool barn, melting in his embrace.

Lila whimpered and Dan was energized. This woman brought out his passion, his kindness, his tenderness. He'd never known anything like this. He deepened the kiss, wanting to be even closer, the explosion of senses threatening to bring him to his knees.

Shyly, Lila reached her arms around his neck to play with the hair at his collar. Bravely, she participated in the kiss, enjoying the warmth of his body. *Please don't let this be a dream.* At that thought, she kissed him harder.

She was killing him. That was all there was to it. He had to ease back before he wouldn't be able to stop. Slowly he pulled away, breaking contact, and rested his forehead against hers. He took a deep breath and said, "Lila, you're incredible. That was—"

The shrill ring tone of his cell phone interrupted the tender scene. Recognizing who was calling, Dan stepped back. "I'm sorry, I have to take this." Lila nodded and headed to the other side of the barn to give him some privacy.

"Hello, Sarah? I'm still in Vermont. The blizzard's over thankfully but it's still going to be a couple of days before I can get out." There was a pause as he listened. "I'm hanging in there. Not much to do but enjoy the snow." Another pause.

"Yeah. Lucky you in Florida." Somberly he said, "How is he?" He listened to the report and reiterated that he'd be there as soon as he could.

After ending the call he looked around the barn. "Lila?" She was gone. Now where could she be? And just when things were beginning to get interesting. He thought maybe it was time to tell her about Sarah and Russell. He wanted to talk to Lila, needed to talk to Lila, hear her thoughts. He simply wanted to be with her, hear her laughter and her voice.

He sighed. Could it be that he was falling in love with Lila Benson?

"So, you've got the change in my reservations then? I'll be arriving the thirtieth of December instead of the twenty-sixth." Richard was on his cell phone to a luxury hotel in St. Tropez trying to get his reservations straightened out since the blizzard had changed his plans. "Thank you very much."

"Why can't we go with you, Dad," Kevin asked as his father clicked off his phone.

"Because it's my vacation before I have to go back to work." Seeing the disappointed look on his son's face, he said, "Hey, we've had a great time here. I'll be with you Christmas Day. Then you get to spend the rest of your vacation with your mom. Sounds fun to me." Richard reached around Kevin's head to ruffle his hair.

"I guess so."

"But Daddy, why do you have to go so far away from us to have a good time? Don't you like us anymore?" Jenna asked.

Richard turned to Celia who was working on Jenna's angel costume. She glanced up at him as she worked, her expression saying, "You're not getting any help from me."

He sat on the edge of one of the beds and reached for his kids. They sat beside him as he spoke. "Guys, I love you. It's just that . . ." He wanted to say that since he was almost a free man, he wanted to travel and see the world. But that would sound too crass. He wanted to explain about adults and their relationships, but that was too complicated. He wasn't even sure he understood them. Looking into the questioning eyes of his children, his flesh and blood, he felt like scum from the bottom of the pond outside. They looked to him and he knew they felt let down. He had to fix this, but how?

"Tell you what. You let me have this one vacation by myself, and at spring break I'll take you to Disney World." That should do it.

"Disney World? All four of us?" Kevin asked.

"Gee, Dad, that's great! Did you hear, Mom? We're all going to Disney World!" Jenna exclaimed.

"Whoa, whoa, whoa. I said I'd take you two. I'm sure that your mother will have other plans." His eyes implored Celia to tell them she had other plans. When she said nothing, Richard turned back to his kids and said, "Say, how about you two go set up the Chinese checkers for a game after dinner?" Complying with his wishes, Kevin and Jenna left the suite.

"You know, you could have helped me out with that," Richard said through his gritted teeth.

"Why? I think you were handling it just fine," Celia said, her eyes on her sewing.

"Sure you do. I can tell by that muscle twitching in your neck. You think this is all fine and dandy." Richard stood up and walked to stand in front of her, his arms folded. "If you've got a problem with this, I'd like to hear it."

Chuckling, Celia said, "Oh, no. I don't think you would."

"Come on, Celia. The kids aren't here. What's on your mind?"

She looked up. As calmly as she could, she set her sewing to the side. She gripped the arms of the chair to settle herself. "Okay, if that's what you want. I agree with the children about this trip to St. Tropez. I can't believe you're leaving them during the holidays to go party on the French Rivera."

"What's so bad about it? I *am* spending Christmas with them. Why can't I spend a little time on myself? I've always wanted to go there."

Celia's mind was exploding. "What? Since when? In the entire time that I've known you, I have never heard you say you wanted to go to St. Tropez!"

"It just came up!" Richard yelled back.

I'll just bet. Who are you meeting there, Richard? "Well why can't you go when the kids are in school? You can go halfway around the world anytime you want."

"For you information, it isn't halfway around the world. And I think getting off by myself would energize me, make me a better father."

"Oh, what a croc. It's an excuse, just like everything else you've been telling your children for the past several months."

"Really? Like what?"

"Like everything is going to be okay. Things are going to get better. You'll still see them as often after the divorce is final."

"Well, I will!"

"Not when you're flying across the ocean to spend a fortune to lie out on some beach with topless women all around you!" Celia grabbed a breath and continued. "You don't want to deal with the problems that your children will face with the divorce. Real problems that you're leaving me to work through. Richard, they're going to need help getting through this. I don't know if I can . . ." Celia's eyes filled and she quickly turned away.

Richard didn't know what to do. "Celia."

She hurried into the bathroom and slammed the door, leaving him standing there.

Outside the suite, tears streamed from Jenna's eyes. Kevin put his arm around her as he led her downstairs, wiping a stray tear from his own eyes.

Dinner was a quiet affair. Tension filled the air, thicker than Mary's Santa stew. No one was talking. Richard and Celia weren't talking. Jenna and Kevin picked at their food, their eyes on their plates. Lila wasn't talking or looking at Dan, who was equally quiet. Mary set out the food, fighting a terrible headache. She asked Angela if she could take over for her while she went to her apartment and checked on Bradley. Joe was nowhere around.

Bo was fully engaged with his food, savoring every bite of the delicious stew. Genevieve blotted her mouth daintily as she worked on her salad, occasionally looking around at the group.

Sam and Eldon ate quietly, every so often exchanging glances with Angela. She was concerned for the people sitting around the table. The hurt that she saw on the faces touched her. She wanted so much to help but she knew that everyone had a free will. They were free to love whomever they chose. She could push and pull and finagle. But in the end, they would make their own decisions.

After Angela served dessert, a coconut cake, and coffee, Joe stuck his head in the dining room and announced, "The lounge will be open tonight. Ten o'clock." A cheer went up from the adults.

"And if you get hungry later, Mary left a few sandwiches in the refrigerator, ham with cheese and turkey. Help yourselves," Angela said.

And then for the first time since the guests had been at the little inn, Angela left the table first.

On the way out of the dining room, Richard's phone signaled a text. Reading it, he smiled and whispered, "Yes!"

"Good news?" Celia asked as they walked down the hall.

"Everything's set for France." He saw the children's faces close up. He stopped and kneeled in front of them. "But we're still going to have fun while we're here, right kids?"

"Oh, will you give it a rest, Richard? All they know is that their dad is leaving them. Is that so difficult to understand?"

"All *I* know is that they have a mother who delights in poisoning their minds against me. Are you happy, Celia?"

"No! As a matter of fact, I haven't been happy since you started working extra hours at night." Celia used her fingers to put air quotes over the last part of her sentence.

"You never did trust me, Cee. Maybe that's what broke us up."

"What bimbo are you meeting in St. Tropez? And does your current girlfriend know?"

Richard took a moment to absorb the accusation. "You're something else, you know that? I know you don't believe me, but I never cheated on you when we were together, Celia." She laughed mockingly. "Besides, I have a feeling Genevieve wouldn't have a hard time about it. We're both young, healthy, . . . single adults."

The comment hurt. Celia stared at Richard and said, "Who are you?" When there was no snappy comeback, she said, "I just don't know you anymore."

Uncomfortable, he said, "Maybe we should just give it a rest. I promised the kids Chinese checkers, isn't that right guys?" Richard and Celia turned, glancing around them but the children weren't there. "Where are they?"

"They probably didn't want to hear us argue."

"That's right," Angela said as she joined them in the hall. The kind, happy face was gone and in its place was a disapproving, hard expression. "You'll find them in your suite, probably crying. Again. For some reason children don't like to hear their parents take each other apart. They want the two most important people in their lives to at least show respect for one another. To act like . . . grownups." Angela walked past them. "That's the least you can do for your own precious children, I'd think."

Jenna and Kevin were in the suite and Richard and Celia could tell they had been crying. Both children declined games in the parlor and instead decided to go to bed.

Richard kissed them and headed out. He had to get away from Celia or he was afraid they'd argue again. Why was it difficult to even talk to her anymore?

After he left, Celia helped the kids get ready for bed. As they lay in their beds reading, Celia sat in the comfy armchair and sewed. All three looked through tears in their eyes.

In the kitchen, Mary put coffee and water in the machine and set the timer. She reached into the upper cabinet and pulled out the aspirin, taking two with a glass of water.

"Still have a headache, I see," Joe said as he came in and opened the drawer of dishtowels.

"Did you need something?" Mary said in a small voice.

"Just a towel for the bar."

"Oh, I think I have some clean ones in the laundry room." Mary turned to go there.

"It's all right. Don't bother." Joe grabbed what he wanted and started to leave the room.

"Joe." He stopped in his tracks at his name on her lips. "Are you serious about quitting?"

Looking down and twisting the towel, just like his gut was doing, he answered, "Yeah."

"But why?" Mary asked with pleading eyes. "Don't you know that we need you around here? Angela, Bradley, . . . me."

Joe shook his head. "No. You don't. Any handyman will do. I'm sure you won't have trouble finding a replacement."

"No one can replace you, Joe. You must know that. Especially with Bradley. He thinks you're the greatest thing ever. How can you leave him?"

Joe's dark eyes pinned Mary. "Do you think I want to leave? Do you think it's not tearing me apart to think of saying goodbye to Bradley . . . and you? But Mary you've made it very clear that there can never be anything more between us. I can't go back. I love you too much."

"Joe—"

"No, no more talk. Let me leave while I still have at least a little pride left." Almost tearing the towel in two, he left the room, leaving a miserable Mary behind. How was she going to explain this to Bradley? He'd already lost the most important man in the world to him and now he was losing another.

Because she was a coward.

Dan hated love. Maybe this was why he had avoided it for so many years. He watched Lila ignore him as she looked through the books in the parlor. She chose one and started out. Seeing this as his chance, he took her arm and led her into the hall.

"Would you kindly let go of my arm," Lila said.

"After you tell me what happened. We were getting along so well in the barn and then I turn to find you gone. Lila, talk to me." Dan hated that he sounded desperate.

"I just figured that you wanted to be alone to take your call."

"No, that's not it. You've avoided me like the plaque since then. I want to know what's changed."

Tears started to pool in Lila's eyes. "Nothing's changed. Nothing at all."

Now Dan was beyond frustration. "Why is it that women think they have to talk in code?"

"Because men are usually too stupid to pick up simple words. I meant, nothing about us has changed, and yes I mean nothing. Does that answer all of your questions, Dan?"

"Well, you're wrong. Something has changed. Lila, I . . . have feelings for you. I want to be your friend, yes, but I want to be more than that. I thought you were feeling the same way."

Lila laughed without any real humor, looking straight ahead. "You know, I used to dream of you saying those words to me. Funny, I never expected to be so confused when you said them." Turning to Dan she said, "I am just getting to the point where I really believe in myself. The last thing I need is for . . . for . . . you to come along and break my heart."

"I won't," Dan said.

Lila knew that he already had and would probably do it over and over if she let him. Taking a deep breath she said the words that had devastated her years before. "You know that there could never be anything between us, don't you?"

Chapter Fourteen

Celia was hungry. She hadn't been able to eat much at dinner and her stomach was now reminding her of that fact. She slipped past her sleeping children and headed downstairs to the kitchen and the sandwiches Angela had spoken of.

Pulling a turkey sandwich from the refrigerator, she set it on the counter and checked its contents. *Needs more mayo.* Since there was none in the refrigerator, Celia walked into the pantry to find a new jar. As she was there, she heard voices coming into the kitchen.

"You go ahead, Richie. I'm not really hungry. I'm afraid I've gained five pounds since I've been here."

"Well, you don't look like it."

Celia heard a giggle follow the comment as she realized who was in the other room. She was trapped, not wanting to see the pair but yet dreading hearing what was going on between them. Her heart pounded in her chest and her breath caught in her throat. Could she endure anymore difficulties with Richard in one day?

Now she had to listen to "Richie" whisper sweet nothings to his new girlfriend.

"Maybe you'd like to find out."

Celia heard the refrigerator slam. "What?"

There was a sigh and then Genevieve's softly purring voice. "Why don't you come up to my room?"

It was quiet for a moment and Celia tried not to think about what was happening in the next room. She shouldn't be there. Why was fate so harsh with its reality? Was she really supposed to hear all this? She stuck her fingers in her ears and closed her eyes hard trying to imagine being anywhere else but where she was at the moment.

Unfortunately, it didn't work. As if her ears were set to fine tuning, she could have heard a pin drop from across the building.

"I have a beautiful, romantic room. It's set in . . . I think Angela said someplace called 'Whoville,' a Christmas village somewhere. And there are these silly little statues of a green Santa all around the room."

Richard chuckled. "The Grinch Who Stole Christmas" was one of their kids' favorite Christmas stories. Was he thinking about the children? "Genevieve. I don't think that would be a good idea."

"Why not? The kids are probably sound asleep by now. They wouldn't have to know."

How could Richard even think about sleeping with another woman when the kids were a few doors down? Would he be doing that when the divorce was final? Celia held her breath trying not to make a sound, to steady her racing heart.

Richard sighed. "I just don't think it would be appropriate." After another pause, he said, "How about we meet up in New York after I get back from Europe. Then we'll have plenty of time to get to know each other, take things slow and easy."

Celia barely heard the footsteps leading out of the kitchen. Her quiet sobs were becoming uncontrollable. She grabbed her stomach and bent over, smothering her mouth with her hands. The pain was unbearable. She slid to the floor and sat there quietly in her anguish.

A few minutes later, the pantry door opened and Celia felt someone sit down next to her. Looking up, she saw the tender eyes of Angela. The woman took Celia into her arms and held her tightly. Giving up all pretense of decorum, Celia let go and wept bitterly in the arms that held her.

The next morning was Christmas Eve. The breakfast crowd was light. The adults all seemed to want to skip the meal and sleep in. Kevin told Angela that both his parents had murmured that they needed more sleep and to go to breakfast without them. Lila had sent word that she wasn't hungry and wouldn't be eating. Dan had consumed a few too many drinks the previous night and was undoubtedly enduring a hangover. Bo and Genevieve were nowhere to be seen.

Angela sat at the table with Kevin and Jenna, Bradley, Sam, and Eldon. Eldon seemed to be the only one with an appetite that morning. The children merely played with their food while Sam and Angela exchanged concerned expressions.

Finally, Angela said, "Your breakfast all right this morning, kids?"

She was answered with muffled approval and a "great" from Eldon.

There was silence again until Jenna said, "Thank you for breakfast, Miss Angela but I'd like to be excused now."

"What's wrong with you children? Usually you've got an appetite like a herd of elephants in the morning."

The three children looked at each other not knowing what to say. Then little Bradley spoke up. "We're mad!"

"Mad?"

"Yeah, we're ticked off. We believed and things are worse than before," Kevin explained to her.

Jenna turned to Sam. "You said we should believe, Sam. I'm afraid if we believe any harder, something terrible will happen, like Mom and Dad will send us away to a boarding school or something."

"Yeah, and replace us with Ginger."

"Ginger?" Angela was confused.

"I'll explain later," Sam said.

Angela's heart was heavy. How should she handle this? Before she could say anything, Sam said, "There's something you should know about belief, kids. You believe that what's meant to happen will happen. You hope for the best but we don't always know what the best is."

"That sounds like a grownup cop-out," Kevin said.

"Maybe. But if we didn't believe and hope for things, what kind of world would this be?"

"But you're Santa!" Hands up in a pleading position, Bradley tried to make his case. "We wished on a falling star, it's Christmas, and you came? Shouldn't we get our wish?"

"Kids, I tried to tell you I'm not Santa. I'm just a guy traveling through." Sam looked at Angela for help.

"Grownups. They're a screwy bunch," Eldon chimed in.

Another moment of silence passed before Angela spoke. "I think the problem is where you have your belief."

"What do you mean, Miss Angela?" Jenna asked.

Smiling, Sam said, "I think what she means is that we need to take these concerns to a higher authority."

"Higher than Santa?" Bradley asked with wide eyes.

"Much higher." Angela folded her hands on the table, bowed her head and closed her eyes. Sam and Eldon followed suit. Jenna looked at the boys, folded her hands, and bowed her head. Bradley shrugged and followed, as did Kevin.

The prayer from Angela sounded like music to the children. They could barely hear the words for the melodic cadence and comforting tone. A deep peace settled over the room by the time Angela said "Amen."

"Now eat, kids. I think you're going to need all your strength."

Everyone went back to their plates of food, thinking. Bradley looked up and asked, "Miss Angela? Can my daddy see me?"

"Oh, Bradley, dear. I'm sure he knows all about you and is so proud."

"I want to be just like him, you know."

With a knowing smile, Angela said, "And so you shall, sweet Bradley."

After breakfast, the children went off to play while Angela helped Mary clean up. "Are you feeling better today?" she asked Mary.

"Yes, thank you," Mary whispered.

Turning to her, Angela said, "We had a very quiet breakfast this morning."

"Yes. It seems that everyone wanted extra sleep. Or just didn't want to see each other." Mary sighed. "I'll be glad when the weather clears a little more and everyone can leave."

"Everyone?"

Mary's eyes went to Angela's. "You probably already know. Joe gave me his resignation yesterday, effective February first. He, ah, wants to travel, find other jobs to do. I think I should tell him that two weeks notice is soon enough. I mean if he wants to go he should go. Not hang around here, miserable." Mary's voice choked on the last word and Angela walked over to her.

"There's more to the story than you're telling me. Isn't there?"

Mary couldn't keep the tears from streaming down her cheek. She couldn't speak so she nodded.

Angela led her to the kitchen table and made tea, setting it along with a small plate of chocolate chip cookies on the table. When Mary saw the cookies, she couldn't help smiling.

"So, did you tell Joe that you're in love with him?"

Mary shook her head. "I can't ask him to settle for me. He's too much of a man, to . . ." She sighed heavily. "He's too wonderful to give up what he wants in life to be saddled with me."

"Now what are you talking about?"

Mary looked deeply into Angela's eyes. "You know exactly what I'm talking about."

Angela quietly said, "Don't you think Joe has the right to decide for himself what he wants?"

Taking a sip of tea, Mary shrugged. "I suppose he does."

"Is it that you're afraid of him leaving after you tell him? Or are you afraid of him staying?"

Pain gripped Mary's chest—a pain she hadn't experienced since she was told that her beloved husband had been killed. The grief was so consuming, she was sure she was going to die from it. "Angela," Mary whispered before dissolving into sobs.

Angela rushed to her side and held her. The deep sobs stirred her heart as she rocked Mary back and forth and waited for the woman to expend her grief.

Mary sighed. "I love him, you know. I love him so much I ache with it."

"Well, for goodness sakes, tell him. He's not a mind reader, you know."

Mary couldn't help it. With all the times that Angela had simply known things, here she was telling her that Joe wasn't like that. She laughed.

Angela lifted Mary's chin with a finger and looked her squarely in the eyes. "What are you waiting for?"

Mary started to answer when she heard a scream come from outside.

Dan lay face down in his bed. He tried to open one eye but was assaulted with brilliant white all over the room. Oh yeah, he thought. He was in the "White Christmas" room. Everything was done in white with a few brief touches of mountain green and sky blue. The brilliance of the white caused his head to pound harder.

Slowly and with great care, he rose and walked to his bathroom where he pulled some aspirin out of his shaving kit and swallowed them with water from the tap. He looked at himself in the mirror. The clothes that he had not bothered to change last night were wrinkled beyond description. His hair was standing straight up. Dark smudges were under his eyes making him look years older. "You are a handsome devil," he said sarcastically to himself. "No wonder Lila can't stand the sight of you."

Walking back into his bedroom, he spied his cell phone on the dresser. He hadn't heard anything since yesterday morning. He had to find out. Walking over to grab the phone he thought about his behavior since being at the inn. He never drank that much. Even in times of stress, he wasn't generally a drinker. But now, he seemed to need something to calm him, to numb him so he turned to alcohol.

He really wanted to turn to Lila.

His thoughts went again to the woman who seemed to invade every waking and non-inebriated moment of his time. How would she react to the news? He knew. She would be sympathetic, kind. Would she be forgiving, that was the question.

Dan punched in the number and waited. Upon hearing voice mail, he said, "Sarah, call me." Then he punched in his parents' phone number and waited. A scream from outside had him clicking off and running for the back door of the inn.

Jenna was screaming for all she was worth as people came running from the inn, the barn, and the shed.

Joe arrived first and sized up the situation. He saw Kevin standing by the edge of the frozen pond, dangerously close to where a part of the ice had broken and water was churning. Close to him, he saw a head in the water, mumbling to Kevin to back away. He sprinted to the pond.

Angela arrived next and ran to Jenna. "What happened, child?" Jenna's crying was hysterical and Angela couldn't understand her. "Now Jenna. Listen to me. Take a breath and tell me what happened."

The authority in Angela's voice made her stop and clearly speak. "We were playing ball. Dad was throwing the ball and Kevin and I were taking turns catching. The ball went over Kevin's head out onto the frozen pond and he ran to get it." She began sobbing again. "He didn't see the cones. He walked past them and we started to hear loud noises. Daddy yelled and ran for him and pushed him away and then Daddy fell in." Jenna bawled. "I don't know what to do?"

As Sam, Eldon, Bo, and Dan joined Joe at the pond, Angela wrapped the girl in her arms and said, "Your yelling was exactly the right thing to do, sweet girl. You just hang on tight to me."

Joe immediately lay down on his stomach by the edge of the break in the ice. "Come on, Richard, grab my hand." Joe felt someone grabbing his feet and looked back to see Sam lying on his stomach holding Joe. Eldon joined the chain, followed by Bo and Dan. Confident that he could now use all his strength to pull Richard up,

Joe stretched out both hands and taking Richard's freezing hands pulled with all his might.

Frightened and unsure, Kevin gingerly walked back to lie down and take Dan's legs. Dan looked back at him and gave him a nod and a wink.

The women had all come out of the house and quickly accessing the situation, Mary went back into the house to make more coffee.

Celia went back in and gathered up the thickest, warmest wool blanket she could find. By the time she was out of the inn, they had Richard out of the pond. Joe had his arms around Richard walking him toward the building. Celia ran to them and wrapped the warm blanket around her husband, leading him in the back door.

Hearing them come in, Mary called out, "Celia, go ahead and get him upstairs. I'll bring a pot of coffee up."

"Thanks."

Richard's lips were blue and his teeth were chattering together as he tried to communicate with Celia. In their suite, she led him to the bathroom and started a hot bath. She turned back to Richard and took the blanket. As he stood there shivering, she started to undress him. Richard had the presence of mind to object.

"C-c-celia. D-d-d-don't."

"Oh, for heaven's sake, Richard. I'm a nurse. Now I'm going to get you into this hot tub and then I'm going to get your bed ready for you. I have a feeling you have a bad cold coming in your near future."

As if to put an exclamation point to her prediction, Richard let out a loud sneeze.

"God bless you."

Mary brought the hot coffee up and left, promising hot chicken soup for Richard's lunch. Celia thanked her and got out Richard's pajamas and heavy socks. After giving him time to warm up in the tub, she walked back into the bathroom to help him get out and get dressed.

Richard was warm. In fact, he was almost hot at her appearance. "Do you mind?"

"No, not at all," Celia said casually as she reached for a towel. "You should get out of the tub now. Don't want to let the water get too cool and chill you. Mary brought some coffee and I want you to take some extra-strengthed pain reliever before you get back into bed."

Ever since last night Richard had been on edge. The encounter with Genevieve in the kitchen had stunned him. He'd realized he wasn't ready to be with another woman. As she'd been propositioning him, all he could think of was Celia. The kids. Their life together. The words of Joe kept ringing in his ears. Was he really making a mistake? No, he'd run everything through his mind so many times. It all made sense.

Except for the look in his kids' eyes. The sadness emanating in Celia. And the hollowness in his soul. Maybe that was why he wanted to run off to Europe, to fill the void.

After a restless night he thought he'd get some fresh air with the kids, clear his mind. Now he was cold, achy, and vulnerable. Not the position he wanted to be in with Celia. "And just who made you my personal nurse?"

"I took on the position myself."

"Yeah, well, you can just forget it. Just leave me alone. I don't need you." Richard stood to take the towel and suddenly felt all kinds of aches and pains jolt through his body. He began to moan as he tried to dry himself.

The words had hurt Celia. She had felt the impact of them for months but now for Richard to verbally say those things to her pierced her heart. Nurse attitude, she told herself. Richard needed her help as a nurse, whether he believed it or not. She would have to live with his not needing her as his wife.

She took the towel, dried him off, and helped him into his pajamas. She guided him to the bed and helped him climb in. Without a word, Celia got the medicine and gave it to him along with a glass of water. He was in too much pain to object. Before she put on his thick socks, she took his feet, one at a time, and rubbed them to bring some warmth and increase the circulation. Satisfied that they were heating up, she slipped on his thick socks and pulled the cover over him.

Richard was breathing hard, the full impact of his ordeal catching up to him. Celia leaned over and whispered into his ear. "Drink some coffee and get some rest. I'll be back to check on you later."

His answer was a sneeze and a moan.

Back in the kitchen, Mary had made another pot of coffee as several others waited to hear how Richard was doing. The kids sat at the table, each with a cup of hot chocolate, waiting. When Celia came into the kitchen, Kevin jumped up, scared out of his wits. "Is he going to be okay?"

Celia smiled at her son and went to him, giving him a big hug. "Of course, he is, honey. He's resting now and he'll probably have a killer cold, but he's going to be just fine."

Tears filled the young boy's eyes. "I froze, Mom. I didn't know what to do. Something could have happened to him."

"Don't you worry about your father. He's a smart guy. He knows how to take care of himself in an emergency."

"He pushed me away so that I wouldn't fall through. But then he fell in instead." A tear slipped from Kevin's control and slid down his face.

Celia lifted Kevin's face to hers. "Well, I guess that makes your dad a hero, huh?" After another smile, she hugged him tighter.

"I think this calls for a celebration. Mary, how about we make maple crème brulee for tonight's dessert?" Angela asked.

"Crème brulee? That's Richard's favorite," Celia said. Mary smirked at Angela. "But could you leave off the nutmeg? He's allergic."

"Absolutely. I think our kitchen blowtorches are packed in the shed. Lila could you look for them please? I'll get Dan to help you." As Lila started to protest, Angela continued speaking. "It's in a box marked kitchen equipment. It may be up on the highest shelf but I'm sure that Dan will be able to reach it. Thank you so much, dear."

Feeling railroaded, Lila gave a slight smile and headed out the back door. She walked over to the shed, hearing Dan's boots crunching snow behind her. She was going to quickly find the box and get back to the inn. Maybe go to her room and write in her journal. Anything to get away from Dan Hamilton. He was poison to her and she wasn't taking it.

In the shed, Lila rubbed her arms for warmth and started looking around at the boxes. She hadn't remembered there being quite so many. The boxes were on four long shelves, the highest near the ceiling. A stepladder was folded in the corner, but Angela had been right. If the box was on the highest shelf, she couldn't reach it.

"Wow. That's a lot of boxes," Dan said as he surveyed the situation.

"I guess we'd better start looking." Lila walked to the other side of the shed, as far away from Dan as she could.

They worked in silence for a while until she suddenly got very excited. "Oh, I think I see it. Look up there," she said, pointing as Dan walked over. On the top shelf was a box marked kitchen equipment.

"Looks like it," Dan agreed and got the stepladder out and adjusted it. He stepped as high as he could and reached up. It still was a little higher and he stretched up on his toes to reach it.

"Be careful, Dan," she said without thinking.

He smiled as he reached further. His fingers inched the box away from the shelf before he was able to get a good grasp of it. As his hands took purchase, he edged the box closer, prepared for the weight of it. And was surprised when the lightweight box flew out of his hands. He reached for it as it fell and in the process, fell himself, hitting the ground with a loud thump.

"Oh!" Lila said, running to bend over him. "Are you all right?"

Her bright, caring eyes looking into his, he didn't know if he'd ever be all right again. He would admit it now. He was undeniably in love with Lila Benson.

When he didn't answer but continued staring at her, Lila repeated her question. "Dan, are you all right? Did you hurt yourself?"

"Huh? No, no. I'm all right." He brushed off his pants as he stood. "My pride's a little hurt but that's all."

Lila giggled as she reached to retrieve the small equipment that had fallen out of the box. Dan joined her, grinning at her giggles. Should he take the chance of talking to her? She had completely shut him down before. Would she do it again?

The chance was taken from his hands as Lila walked to the door with the box. She wasn't going to give him any chances. He understood that. She pulled on the doorknob and nothing happened. She pulled again. Setting the box down, she pulled with both hands but the door did not budge.

They were trapped inside.

Chapter Fifteen

"I think I've got some Bengay here." Angela was on the third floor, in her small apartment searching her medicine cabinet. "Yes, here it is. Please, take it and use all you need with Richard."

"Thank you. I'm sure when he wakes up from his nap his muscles are going to be killing him."

"What a good thing that he has you to take care of him."

Celia looked down at the tube of ointment. "Yes," she murmured. "Well, thank you again, Angela."

She started toward the door when Angela stopped her. "You've been a nurse for how long?"

"I started before the kids were born. Probably about a dozen years or so, why?"

Ignoring the question, Angela continued. "And I bet you've had your share of hurting patients."

"I could write a book."

"I'm sure you could." Angela touched her arm gently. "Remember when you're treating Richard that he's hurting." Celia was puzzled. "I'm sure he doesn't really mean all he's saying to you. It's just the pain talking."

Celia's eyes went back to stare at the ointment. In a small voice she said, "I don't know. He probably means everything he's saying to me."

"I doubt that very much. But as a nurse I'm sure you understand the power of kindness. You know, Celia, it's the same in a marriage." She looked at Angela as the woman continued. "I mean, we're so careful to be kind to strangers that sometimes we end up not being so kind to those closest to us. It's been my observation that a little bit of kindness, whether it's in word or deed, can go a long way."

Angela squeezed Celia's arm. "Even to a husband. Even to an ex-husband."

Celia thought about that for a second. "You're right, Angela. I will be kind to Richard." She opened the door to walk through it. "Even if it kills me."

Angela chuckled. "I have a feeling that kindness is just what you two need. You be the first and watch what happens."

Celia continued to think about this as she went down the stairs to their suite. She would sit and wait for him to wake up and then rub some ointment on him—all the while being kind.

However, the thoughts flew from her head as she heard the soft giggling of Genevieve coming from inside their suite.

"What's wrong?" Dan asked coming up behind Lila.

"I can't open the door."

"Here, let me see." He pulled, getting the same result. "That's strange."

He continued to try and Lila found herself backing up. She did not want to be too close to this man. His scent was forever embedded into her memory, causing unwanted reactions in her body. Then she would remember his arms around her, his kisses.

Oh, it would not be good to be trapped in the shed with Dan Hamilton. Lila reached in her pockets looking for her phone. She remembered her phone was in her purse. She hadn't used it since she had gotten to the inn. "Use your phone to call the inn," she suggested.

Dan reached into his pockets and shook his head. "My phone's in my room."

She was starting to get worried and, going to the door, started pounding. "Help! Help us! Somebody!"

Watching with curiosity, Dan said, "Hey, it's okay. They know where we are. Someone will figure it out and come get us." He came up behind her and rubbed her arms. "Are you claustrophobic?"

Only with you. "No. I just have things to do, you know. I don't have time to sit here in this shed."

"It doesn't look like we have a choice for a little while." *Thank you, God.* He pulled out a folding chair and held it for her.

As she sat she said, "Don't you think we should keep yelling?"

"Why? I'm sure it won't be long before they come to get us."

It was quiet as Dan set up a chair for himself while Lila sat looking down at her fidgeting hands. He glanced around for something to talk about. What he really wanted was to ease into talking about Russell. Lila knew Russell. She'd probably want to hear about him.

Finally, Dan took a breath. "You know, I've really got to get down to Florida."

"Yes. I know Sarah is waiting."

"How do you know about Sarah?"

"I heard you on the phone." She stood and paced the shed. "She must be a special woman."

Dan smiled. "She is."

Lila's heart plummeted. "Well, I'm sure you'll be able to get out of here soon and get to her."

"I just hope I can before it's too late." Dan's expression hardened.

"Too late? What, she's going to dump you and find someone else? Boy, Dan you sure know how to pick 'em."

He looked at her with confusion and walked to her. "Why would my best friend's wife dump me?"

Celia didn't know what to do. The door was closed. Should she knock? No, darn it, it was her suite too. *All right, Celia. Think kindness.* Without a thought to what was happening inside, Celia opened the door and went in. Richard lay on the bed, his face contorted in pain. Genevieve sat in a chair next to the bed telling Richard a story of shopping in Hong Kong, where the star of the tale was, of course, her. She was obviously enjoying herself, probably thinking she was cheering Richard up.

Celia could see by his expression that he would have rather been at the dentist than where he was at the moment. She hid a smile as she came in the room. "Hello, Genevieve."

"Hi. I thought I'd check on the bad boy, here. Thought you could sneak in a little swim, did you, huh?"

When he cringed, she could have cheered. She knew that expression and Genevieve was definitely not making a good impression at the moment.

Celia came around to the other side of the bed and gently felt his head for fever. Satisfied that there was none, she felt his hands and moved the cover back to remove his socks and feel the temperature of his feet.

Genevieve sat on the bed and tried to rub Richard's shoulder. His loud moan stopped her. "What's the matter?"

"I hurt all over. What are you trying to do?" Richard gasped through his pain.

Clearly confused by his reaction, Genevieve tried to explain. "I thought I'd massage your shoulders. Make you feel better."

"I really don't want to be touched."

"Well, she's touching you," Genevieve said.

"She's a qualified caregiver. You're not." Genevieve showed her best pouty face and sat back down.

"How's the head? Do you need a stronger pain reliever?" Celia gently asked.

"No, the head's better. My body just aches all over," he murmured.

"I've got some ointment to use whenever you're ready," Celia said.

"Ooooh, can I do it, Richie?"

"No!" Richard's exclamation took the women by surprise. In a quieter voice he said, "Thanks, Genevieve but I think Celia should do this."

One brow raised, Genevieve said, "Well, don't let me keep you." With that she stomped out of the suite.

Richard and Celia watched her go. With no emotion, he said, "How about that ointment, Cee? I don't think my body can wait."

"Let me just warm it up first and we'll get started." She tried her best not to look elated.

The kitchen smelled heavenly with chicken soup simmering and fresh bread baking. Angela and Mary were busy with dinner preparations when Eldon came in through the mudroom.

"Any of you seen Dasher?" he asked without preamble.

Angela and Mary looked at each other. "No," Mary answered.

"Do you think he wandered off into the woods, Eldon?" Angela asked.

"Not like him," Eldon said as he shook his head.

Joe came into the room at that time, a tool belt slung low on his hips. Without looking at Mary he said, "The toilet in your apartment is fixed. Just needed a new filler float."

Without looking at him, Mary said, "Thanks."

"Hey Joe, you seen Dasher outside of the barn today?"

"No, Eldon. Maybe one of the kids let him out," he said.

"Couldn't be Bradley. He's in the apartment," Mary said.

Joe was starting to get a bad feeling. "He's not there now."

"What?" Mary turned to stare at Joe.

"I've been in your apartment for the past half hour. He wasn't there when I got there and he wasn't there when I left."

Mary's face grew pale. She wiped her hands on a towel and ran up the stairs. "Bradley!"

"Where are the other kids, Angela?" Joe was starting to panic.

"They're in the parlor watching some more of those island videos with Sam. They've been there for the past hour."

Mary came running down the stairs. "Joe! I can't find him anywhere! He's not in the inn and his backpack and Pooh Bear are missing! Where could he be?"

Joe moved to Mary and rubbed her shoulders, a grim expression on his face. "Don't worry, honey, we'll find him." Turning to Eldon, he said, "You said the reindeer's missing?"

"Yeah. Haven't seen him since after breakfast this morning."

"Do you think he left with the reindeer?" Mary asked.

"I don't know but it sounds a little coincidental, don't you think," Joe said.

Concerned, Angela said, "Eldon, why don't you head out and see if you can track the reindeer. Make sure you have your cell phone with you. Mary and Joe why don't you head down the cross-country ski trail. See if you find Bradley there."

Mary walked over to Angela. Taking a breath to calm her nerves she said, "Angela, where is he?" When she tried to deny any knowledge, Mary said louder, "You know. You always know. Tell me where my son is, please!" Mary's voice cracked as Joe stood behind her, his hands on her shoulder.

Angela smiled tenderly at the couple. "Bradley is fine. Just follow the trail and you'll come across him."

Mary and Joe were out the door in a flash.

"Your best friend's wife? Your girlfriend is your best friend's wife?" Lila sat down again. "I never thought you'd stoop that low, Dan Hamilton."

213

Dan thought about that and threw back his head and laughed.

And laughed and laughed.

Lila was starting to get a little annoyed with him until he sat down beside her and put his hand on the back of her chair. "This is priceless, just priceless. Sarah and Russell will get a kick out of this."

"I don't understand."

Before she could voice any more concerns, he turned to her and framing her face with his hands, kissed her fully and deeply. It so stunned Lila that she froze as Dan pulled back.

"My sweet Lila," Dan whispered.

"I . . . I really don't understand," Lila finally said.

He took both her hands in his and said, "There's something I need to tell you." He looked deeply into her beautiful hazel eyes that were now a deep chocolate, took a deep breath, and let it out.

"Do you remember Russell Zimmerman?"

Lila thought hard. "You mean from high school? The 'Zim-man'?" Dan nodded. "You and he hung out together.

"We were best friends. Ever since grade school. Anyway, he went to college, studied accounting, did really well for himself. He moved to Florida and met a nice woman, got married. We've stayed in touch over the years. I'd still consider him to be my best friend."

As Dan considered his next words, Lila said, "So why were you talking to his wife on the phone?"

The carefree, confident expression Dan normally had was gone and in its place was a pain so real that it took Lila's breath away. He squeezed her hands harder as he looked into her eyes. "Russell's been diagnosed with terminal cancer."

"No," she whispered, her heart squeezed.

Moisture appeared in Dan's eyes as he continued. "They had suspected cancer. He went for tests and I told Sarah to call me with the news when she heard. She called me that night when I bought you the drink and said those harsh things. Lila, I wasn't myself. I'd just found out that my best friend was dying with cancer. I wasn't in my right mind."

Lila's heart hurt for this man. Tears were pouring down her cheeks as she gently put her arms around him and held tight. She could feel his body shake as he shed quiet tears. They stayed that way for a long time, holding each other, grieving together.

Finally, Dan looked up. Clearing his throat he said, "Sarah's been keeping me posted on how Russell is. As soon as the roads are clear, I'm heading to Florida to see him."

"Of course," Lila choked. She looked at this man she thought she knew and was blown away by the emotion she felt for him. He was a talented writer, successful in his field. He was handsome and charming. But all of that was inconsequential when a friend was hurting.

She loved him. She could admit that now with complete acceptance. The past was gone and

215

along with that all the baggage that she had chosen to carry. She was sure of herself now and feeling that way, she decided to take a leap of faith, knowing that whatever happened, she would be okay. "Dan, can I go with you to see Russell?"

His sad eyes widened. "You want to come to Florida with me?" She nodded. The heaviness lifted slightly with her request. It was so clear to him that he needed her. He wanted her.

And now, he felt that she was ready to be his. He enfolded her in his arms and snuggled her close to him. Whispering in her ear, he said, "Please come to Florida with me."

He began kissing her ear, her neck, and her throat. The peace that he found with Lila touched his soul, giving him relief from the heartache he had been dealing with. His kisses reached her face, and Lila actively sought his mouth. The attraction that had been simmering between the two ignited into a fire of passion. Neither one seemed to be able to get enough of each other.

Lila was sinking into a warm pool of desire. This was what she had been missing all her life, a man to truly give herself to, to love, to support, to cherish. No matter where life took her and Dan, she was ready for it.

She was ready to give instead of hide.

The ointment was nice and warm as Celia began rubbing it on Richard's body. She had taken his shirt off and was straddling him on the bed as he was on his stomach. Celia massaged his shoulders with the lotion, while Richard moaned in relief, feeling his sore muscles relaxing.

"How does that feel?" she asked as her fingers continued making magic on Richard's body.

"If I couldn't feel any of the pain, I'd think I was in heaven," he mumbled.

Celia chuckled. "Well, you deserve relief for what you did. You're a hero for saving Kevin from falling in the pond."

"Really?"

"Uh-huh. Kevin was feeling really bad, thinking you were hurt because of him but I told him that you were pretty smart when it came to emergencies."

"You said that?"

"Yes. Then we decided that you were, in fact, a hero. Kevin's proud of his dad."

Richard smiled, savoring the word "hero." He wasn't sure what to say. "Wow, that's something."

"It is indeed. In fact, in honor of your heroic effort, Mary and Angela are making crème brulee for dessert tonight, special for the hero."

"If I'd known I'd get crème brulee, I'd've been a hero long before now." Celia gave a short laugh. "Oh, they're not going to use nutmeg, are they?"

"No, I told them you were allergic."

Richard was feeling better by the minute. He lay there as Celia rubbed on more ointment, enjoying everything about the moment—being a hero to his son, crème brulee for dinner, Celia's hands. He turned his head slightly to see her. Soft curls fell around her face as her determined look led her to work on his back. Even as her eyes were intense on the job, there was a softness to them that drew Richard in. When she found an especially tight muscle, she bit her tongue in concentration. Richard smiled, remembering the times he had made fun of that habit.

"Okay, I think I've got your back. How about we do your legs?" As she said this, Celia was gently turning Richard over and pulling his pajama bottoms off. He looked up at her straddling him on the bed. This was strange.

For some reason, Richard was a little shy. He had been married to this woman for twelve years and now he was embarrassed for her to take his pants off.

Seeing the slight blush on his neck, Celia asked, "Is that all right?"

"Yeah," he cleared his throat. "Do what you got to do."

Celia smiled and continued. Richard watched her with fascination. She was a giver, a healer. She hadn't deserved his actions or his harsh words. Taking a breath he said, "I'm sorry."

"What?" Celia looked up, still rubbing his tired muscles.

"I said I'm sorry. I was rude and ungrateful and . . . well, basically a jerk before. When I got out of the pond, I mean." Looking into her curious eyes, he again said, "I'm sorry."

Celia smiled at him, causing his heart to lighten. "I understand. You were in pain, you were freezing, probably still concerned about Kevin."

"Don't let me slide on this, Celia. I'm sorry for lashing out at you. I really didn't mean those things I said. You were only trying to help me. Thank you."

Celia couldn't believe her ears. Richard was not only apologizing for his behavior earlier but also expressing thanks. Angela had been right. A little kindness did go a long way. It was so nice not to be fighting with him. The smile that she gave him was so big, it threatened to break her face. "Okay. Yes, you were a jerk." He chuckled. Softly, she added, "And you're welcome."

Their eyes met and held. Celia held her breath not knowing what to say. Finally he said, "Celia, what went wrong?"

Her hands that had stopped rubbing when accepting his apology, went to work again so her nerves wouldn't show. "I guess what happens to so many other couples. Different interests, different priorities, different 'friends.'"

"What do you mean friends?"

Should she tell him what she knew? Maybe it was time to get it all out in the open. With kindness, she reminded herself. "Richard, I know you weren't working all those nights."

"You do?"

"Yes. Several times I needed to get in touch with you and when you didn't answer your cell, I tried the office. Once I got your boss. He said you had left several hours before." Although her heartbeat was accelerating, dreading what she was going to hear, it was time and she was going to get through this with her integrity in tact. "I'm not asking for explanations. You wanted to know what went wrong with us and that was a big part. I didn't feel that I could trust you anymore."

"Because I didn't tell you where I was?"

She thought about that. "No. Because you lied about where you were."

He mulled that through. She had a point. A good point. His own pride had led them here and what had it gotten him? A trip to St. Tropez alone. Hooray.

As Celia worked on his lower legs, he studied his wife. She really was beautiful, inside and out. She deserved the truth—all of it. "Cee, you're right. I wasn't at the office." He took a deep breath and after letting it out said, "I was in class."

Celia stopped working. She gaped at Richard. "Class?"

"Yeah. I was taking classes at NYU. They have an accelerated masters program in business. The company has a policy that those with masters degrees are promoted before those without." He sighed. "I wanted a promotion."

"Well, why didn't you tell me?"

"Because I felt ridiculous going back to school. I didn't want you or the kids to know that I needed more education. I know it's stupid, but it made me feel . . . I don't know, weak."

Celia sat back on her heels. She was confounded. "You mean all this time you've been taking business classes in college?"

"Yeah. I got two A's and a B last semester. I'm doing okay with it. I've only got a few more classes to take and I'll be done."

So many things were falling into place now. All the late nights he had spent away. His frustration at having to defend where he was. Even his desire to go to St. Tropez during Christmas break made some sort of sense now that she knew he was taking classes.

"I'm hoping that I can work my way up to a vice-president. There's plans of opening offices in New Rochelle and I thought that . . ." Richard stopped. He had been going to say that he wanted to work in New Rochelle to be close to his family but that was a moot point now.

What could Celia say? He was trying to earn a better living. She couldn't fault him for that. She started on his shins and said, "Well, I think that's a great goal. I'm sure you'll achieve it in no time."

"Thanks." Because he couldn't help it, he asked, "Cee, why are we arguing all the time?"

She moved to his feet. Richard had always loved having his feet massaged. Celia enjoyed his quiet whimpers as she thought about what to tell him. Calmly and as sincerely as she could, she said, "I suppose I argue because I'm hurt."

"I never meant to hurt you, not really. Maybe sting you a little," he added with a grin. He sobered and said, "But never hurt you."

Celia looked into his eyes, the deep blue eyes that she had fallen in love with so long ago. "What is it you want now, Richard?"

With a sad grin, he said, "I'm not sure, Cee. I think that's the problem."

Chapter Sixteen

Joe's phone rang as he and Mary were about half a mile down the trail. He answered listening to Eldon relate what he'd found. "He's fine then?" Eldon replied to him. "Okay, we're heading there now."

He clicked off and Mary took his arm. "What?"

"Eldon said Bradley is with Dasher, out at the rest spot on the trail."

"But that's five miles from the inn."

"Yeah. Eldon says Bradley's asleep. With his head resting on the reindeer's back. Little guy's tuckered out."

The uncontrollable relief gushed out of Mary as she grabbed Joe and hugged him with all her might. "Thank God. Thank God." The tears started coming. "I was afraid I was going to lose him. He's all I've got, my baby, my only child."

Joe held Mary tightly, tears threatening his own eyes. "Well, he's all right. Eldon's staying with him until we get there."

Mary broke away from Joe and started wiping her eyes. "When I see him, I'm going to give him a hug so hard, it'll probably break his little ribs. Then I'm going to ground him for life."

Joe took her hand. They started down the trail briskly, eager to see the boy. Something kept playing in the back of his mind, something Mary had said. As they walked, he asked, "Why do you think Bradley ran away?"

"He's been pretty upset about things. I think he's still mad at me for yelling at you."

Keeping her hand in his, he said, "Does he know I'm leaving?"

"I'm not sure. I haven't told him but he could have overheard something. You know how he is." They walked in silence. "Do you really have to go, Joe?"

Looking straight ahead, he said, "It'd probably be for the best."

Mary gathered her courage. She couldn't let him leave without knowing the truth. "Joe, I won't hold you to the February first date. If you'd like to leave before then, you're free to go."

"Nice of you," he murmured.

"But before you go I have a few things to tell you."

When she didn't say anything else, Joe said, "I'm listening."

This was hard. This was so hard. "It's just that . . . you see . . . I . . . Well, Joe, I love you."

He froze in his tracks. After a moment, he turned to gaze at the woman that had starred in his dreams for months. Part of him wanted to hold her and kiss her, but another part wanted to make her pay for taking him through all kinds of hell the past couple of days. "I'm sorry if I have a hard time believing that but your actions don't exactly speak of a woman in love."

Knowing she had some explaining to do and not especially wanting to see his face, she took the lead and started walking down the trail. "When Bradley was born, there were some complications. I started bleeding badly and they had to operate." She waited to see if he had any idea where this conversation was going. When he didn't say anything, she continued. "The operation was pretty massive and they ended up having to take . . . I mean they . . . Okay, I'm just going to say it. I can't get pregnant anymore." Joe was quiet. She stopped and faced him. "Did you hear what I said? I can't bear children."

"Yeah, I heard you. So?"

"So? What do you mean *so*? You love children. You're still a young man. You deserve to find a whole woman, one that can give you a houseful of children. Not someone who has baggage from the past. I love you too much. I want you to have everything you could possibly want in your life?"

"Do you really?" Joe was fuming. He walked right up to her and taking her arms, bent down until his face was a few inches from hers. "Then why are you preventing it?"

"I don't understand."

"*You* are all I want in life. I don't care about more children. I happen to be crazy about the one you've already got!" Mary's eyes searched his for confirmation of what he was saying.

"And how could you think for one second that you're not a whole woman? That's the stupidest thing I've ever heard, and Mary you're not stupid! You're more woman than any I've ever known. You're a great mother, a hard worker, a faithful friend. And you're the sexiest woman I've ever seen stir a pot of stew!" Mary smiled through her tears.

Joe reached his big arms around her and now spoke tenderly. "I just want to be your husband, Mary. And Bradley's stepfather. With that how could I ever want anything else?"

Mary saw Joe's heart in his eyes. She was awed at the intensity of the love there. She gently reached out to stroke his long, lean face—a face she had grown to count on, to love. She was sure that her heart would burst as she realized the deep love they felt for one another. She whispered, "Don't go."

"Marry me," he returned.

A smile broke across Mary's face, threatening to outshine the afternoon sun. With a nod of her head, she threw her arms around his neck and planted a hard kiss on his lips.

Joe drew her closer and took the kiss deeper. He kissed her again and again, his heart light and peaceful for the first time in years. He had everything now.

It took a herculean effort to pull back from her, his fiancée. Smiling down at her, he said, "Let's go get Bradley."

As they walked down the trail, Mary said, "He'll be ecstatic. He already thinks of you as his stepfather."

"Good. I want him to be my best man. Soon."

Richard's mind kept going back to the question Celia had asked. What did he want? He was still thinking about that as Celia sat reading a book. He had told her that he didn't need a nursemaid but she'd insisted on staying, wanting to make sure he was all right.

His eyes caught a book that peeked out from Jenna's suitcase. "What's that?"

Celia looked where he was pointing. "Oh, it's an assignment that Jenna had in school." She reached to pick it up and handed it to him. "They had to put together a scrapbook of favorite Christmases from the past." Celia sat back down with her book.

He starting turning the pages of the homemade book, filled with family photos. "Remember this one?"

She got up to come beside him and looked down at a picture of Jenna's first Christmas. Proud big brother was holding her in front of the Christmas tree and Celia was right next to him to help support the baby. "Yes. I was so scared that Kevin was going to drop her."

Richard chuckled. "He was very proud of his baby sister. That is until she got old enough to get into his stuff." Celia agreed and sat back down.

"What about this one," he said, forcing her to get up again and walk over.

"Oh, yes. The bright green bicycle for Kevin and the hot pink one for Jenna."

Laughing, he said, "Then we had to wait until spring until we could use them."

"At least we had a garage. Remember, you held Kevin on his and I held Jenna on hers and we went in circles for hours, it seemed."

"Yeah. Didn't need to go to the gym that winter." Celia smiled and sat back down.

"Cee, you've got to see this picture."

"For goodness sakes, Richard." She walked back over to him to look at the photo.

"Well, sit down. Look at this with me."

Gingerly, she sat, not wanting to cause any stress to his muscles and leaned down to look at the picture he was looking at.

The grainy picture showed Richard and Celia in front of the Christmas tree, their arms around each other. Kevin was in front of them with his arms folded. Jenna was kneeling by them. All four people were off center and crooked in the picture. Celia started laughing. "I can't believe we kept that picture."

"Do you remember? Kevin was trying out the self-timer on his new camera but he didn't have a tripod. So he put it on the table." Richard started laughing. "The timer worked, but unfortunately the camera was slanted."

They both laughed as they studied the picture. Richard turned the page and they saw the

Christmas that the kids got a puppy. "Aw, Tramp. Hey, who's taking care of Tramp?"

"Kimmie is," Celia said speaking of a neighbor.

"I really miss Tramp."

"He really misses you."

Silence. Richard turned the page. "Hey, what's that on the mantel in this one," Richard asked.

Celia leaned over to get a good look at the picture. The light scent of vanilla that she wore wafted to Richard's nose. He took a sniff enjoying the aroma, remembering all the places and times that went along with it. He was enjoying her nearness.

"I think it's that clock you gave me—the funny one with the nurse holding the thermometer."

"Oh, yeah." He smiled remembering picking that clock out for Celia, knowing that she would get a good laugh at it and think of him whenever she saw it. He wondered where it was now.

Richard continued to turn pages. "You know, we had some really good times."

"Yes, we did," Celia said quietly.

The last page of the book had a picture of Celia and Richard, sitting together on the couch. Jenna was laughing holding mistletoe over their heads and they were smiling, totally involved in a kiss.

Neither one spoke. They were sitting very close together. Celia's leg was against Richard's. She felt a spark go through her body as she remembered what happened later that night after that kiss. She wanted that again but knew it was out of her control. So, she just sat there and waited for Richard to say something, anything.

Finally, he said, "Celia, you asked me earlier what I wanted now."

"Yes."

"I want to kiss you. Right now."

She turned to him, recognizing the hunger, the need, and the want. And felt all those things herself. She stayed where she was, thinking that Richard would surely change his mind any second. But slowly his hand reached up to her cheek and drew back into her hair, gently pulling her head toward his.

Richard's lips were gentle on hers but powerful. After a brief kiss, he looked into her eyes, where tears pooled. He muttered her name and kissed her deeply and satisfyingly. He reached for her and pulled her down across his lap. The kissing went on, each expressing the deep emotion that they felt for each other.

Soon, it wasn't enough. He lay her down on his bed. As he continued to kiss her, he said, "Where are the kids?"

"They're watching DVDs with Sam," she said breathlessly.

He hobbled out of bed, locked the door and got back under the covers, moaning slightly from his aches and pains. "Good," he said as he took her in his arms and kissed her once again.

In between kisses, Celia said, "Are you sure you feel up to this?"

A beautiful smile crossed his lips. "Believe me, Mrs. Davis. I've never felt better."

In the parlor, Sam, Jenna, and Kevin had just learned that bamboo rafts would not get you safely back to Hawaii from a deserted island. Good to know.

"That was a funny one," Jenna said. "I want to go tell Mom the joke about Ginger's dyed hair."

As Jenna got up to head for her parents' room, Sam stopped her. "Why don't we leave them alone a little longer."

Jenna and Kevin just looked at him.

"I mean, so your dad can get better." He didn't want to get their hopes up. "I'm sure they'll be down for dinner. You know we're having a special dessert that Mary and Angela use blowtorches to . . ." Sam slapped his forehead. "The shed!" he cried before he ran out of the room.

Looking around to see if anyone was watching him, Sam pulled out a key. He put the key in the lock that was on the door of the shed and once opening the lock, discretely pocketed both lock and key. He opened the door saying, "We were wondering where you two had . . ." He stopped when he saw what was going on in the shed.

In the back were two folding chairs. Dan was in one with Lila on his lap, the two in the middle of a serious lip lock. "Well, now, just look at the two of you. Yes, I guess all you needed was a little uninterrupted time alone."

They didn't acknowledge Sam's presence but continued in their embrace. For a moment, Sam just stood there watching and sighing.

Vaguely hearing something, Lila looked over. Sam smiled and with his finger next to his nose, winked at her. She winked back and returned her attention to Dan. Sam gently pulled the door to but not closing it so they knew it was open.

Seeing Angela in the kitchen window, he gave her the two thumbs up sign.

As everyone gathered together that night, there was a feeling of excitement. Angela liked to call it "Christmas Happiness." Christmas carols played softly in the background as everyone filled their plate from the buffet and took their seats.

"Well, we've all survived a very memorable day. How are you feeling, Mr. Davis?"

"Angela, after all we've been through, it's Richard. And I'm feeling wonderful." He took Celia's hand and kissed it tenderly. "Thanks to my own private nurse."

Jenna and Kevin's mouths dropped open. They had not seen their parents all day and the change in their attitude was nothing short of a miracle. The kids both looked at Sam and Angela. Sam gave them the signal, which they returned. Angela smiled at them.

"Dan and Lila. I heard about that terrible problem with the shed door. I hope you're not upset about that."

The pair smiled at each other, Dan squeezing Lila's hand under the table. "I somehow think it was a blessing in disguise."

"What happened?" Richard asked.

"It was the strangest thing. We were getting something out of the shed and the door jammed. We couldn't get out until Sam happened by and opened the door."

Everyone looked at Sam who was looking at his plate, busily eating. "Could you pass the bread please, Kevin?"

"And Mr. Bradley. What an adventure you had today."

"Yeah. I was going to join the army just like my dad and Joe when I ran into Dasher in the woods. We were resting when Eldon came by and said I might want to wait until I'm a little older. Mama needs me right now, you know." Bradley took a big bite of mashed potatoes as the adults smiled.

"She absolutely does," Mary said as she brought more homemade bread into the dining room.

Joe was right behind her with a large pitcher of water. "Hey, how about me? I need you to be my best man."

Everyone looked up. Bradley had a grin from ear-to-ear with mashed potatoes all around his mouth. "Yeah! We're getting married!" The congratulations and cheers were deafening.

Hugs and handshakes were passed around as Bradley gave the signal to Sam who returned it with a chuckle. The happy couple was told to sit and join everyone for dinner.

Bradley turned to Angela and asked, "Can we invite the owner of the inn to the wedding?"

Dan was all over that. "Bradley, have you met the owner? Have you seen him?"

Pleased that all the attention was on him, the boy said, "Well, not really. But Angela talks about him all the time. I want him to come see me get married."

Smiling, Angela said, "Of course, dear."

"So, ready to tell us his name, Angela?" Dan turned to her, happy to put her in the hot seat. The others followed his gaze, themselves eager to hear Angela's answer.

She thought about the question for a moment. Leaning over her elbow on the table she looked deeply into Dan's eyes and said, "Who do you think it is Dan?"

Angela's bright blue eyes pinned him. It was as if Angela was looking deeply into his soul, knowing and understanding his entire life. He shuddered. A peace flowed over his head and continued down his body, like a deep and unconditional love. It was unlike anything he'd ever known.

Dan swallowed hard and said, "I don't know."

Smiling widely, Angela said, "Don't worry about it. He'll reveal himself to you when the time's right." She went back to her food as if nothing had happened. "These potatoes are wonderful, Mary."

Conversation continued, light and happy, when suddenly Mary looked around and said, "Where is Genevieve?"

"Yeah, and Bo?" Joe added.

"I believe they've already left." To the questioning looks of the others, Angela said, "It seems that Bo thought the roads were good enough for his SUV and when Genevieve heard that he was leaving, she begged a ride. They left a couple of hours ago."

Celia looked at Richard from the corner of her eyes to see his reaction. When there was none, she relaxed again.

"Gee, I hope they'll be safe," Lila said.

Mary looked at Angela, her brows raised.

Angela returned the look with a smile. "I'm sure they'll be fine."

Dinner continued and when the crème brulee dessert was served, Richard received his plate first to the singing of "For He's a Jolly Good Fellow."

As they were finishing dessert, Richard said, "Angela. Since Genevieve has gone that means you have an extra room." Jenna and Kevin glanced at each other, frowns on their faces.

"Yes, that's right, Mr. Da—I mean Richard. You had wanted a second room. I'll clean the room if you'd still like it."

"Yes, I would."

"Dad, we don't need another room," Kevin said.

"Yeah, I like all four of us being together," Jenna added.

Richard smiled as he stretched his arm over the back of Celia's chair. "Kids, you may like this arrangement."

"Why?" Kevin asked.

"I thought we'd let you and your sister have the suite." His eyes on his wife, he said, "Your mother and I will take the other room."

Chapter Seventeen

After dinner, everyone walked out to the barn for the Christmas program. The children directed Sam, Eldon, Richard, Celia, Angela, and Dan into folding chairs. In the middle of the "stage" were two chairs with a manger in between. With the animals around them, Mary and Joe came out in hastily made Mary and Joseph costumes and sat in the two chairs.

Lila came out with a guitar taken from the music room and softly started strumming "O Little Town of Bethlehem." As she did, she began to read the Biblical account of the very first Christmas. After reading a few verses, everyone joined in singing the song. Lila read again, stopping to sing a solo of "Silent Night."

Dan's eyes glowed with warmth for the woman.

When she got to the part about the shepherds out in the field, little Bradley walked out, in a bathrobe with a towel tied to his head and a large stick. Mary and Joe smiled at each other.

He stood there as Jenna came out in a white sheet fashioned into a gown and a wire hanger bent to sit on top of her head as a halo. In a loud, clear voice, Jenna called out the announcement made by the angels thousands of years ago. Even the animals seemed to be silent as the good news was pronounced. Lila led everyone in singing "Hark the Herald Angels Sing."

As the story progressed, Kevin came out in a purple robe and a construction paper crown to represent the kings that came from the East. He laid a small chest at the foot of the manger and knelt while everyone sang "We Three Kings."

Lila finished the reading and everyone was silent as each one thought about what they'd heard.

Then Angela stood and began to sing "O Holy Night." A glow seemed to surround her face giving her an aura of bright lights, her voice was clear as a bell. No one could look away. When she finished, she sat back down and the barn was again silent while everyone pondered.

Lila strummed the guitar again and everyone sang, "Joy to the World." The show ended and everyone went back to the inn for cider and, what else, cookies. Before long, Mary told Bradley it was time for bed and Celia echoed the sentiment. Only with the prodding of the next morning being Christmas were the kids persuaded to obey without qualms.

Feeling like a part of a big family, Bradley walked around telling everyone goodnight. When he got to Eldon, the man looked at him seriously.

Then he gave him a high-five and a smile. Bradley gave Sam a big hug. "Thank you, Sam. I got just what I wanted for Christmas," he whispered in the man's ear.

"Just remember that we had help, okay?"

"I won't forget."

Jenna and Kevin gave Eldon high-fives and hugged Sam also. Embracing their parents they headed for bed.

Eldon, Sam, and Angela stood watching the children go upstairs. They all three seemed to sigh at once. Breaking the mood, they heard Dan say, "Hey you guys, how about one more cup of cider?"

Bradley woke early the next morning. No surprise there. The sun was just peeking through the mountains as he yelled to his mom that it was Christmas. When he didn't see presents under their little tree in the apartment he frowned.

Trying to open her eyes, she said, "This has been a special Christmas so Santa decided to put your presents downstairs with Jenna and Kevin's."

Bradley was bouncing off the wall with joy. "Oh, boy! It's almost like having a brother and sister. Let's go, Mom!" He pulled on her hand to go downstairs.

"Now just hold on. Let me get dressed and get some coffee in the kitchen downstairs. Then we'll see about the presents."

Sighing dramatically, Bradley waited impatiently for his mom. Once they were in the kitchen she got out several frozen quiches and coffee cakes to heat up for breakfast. Joe came in from feeding the animals. Seeing Mary, he walked to her and kissed her. "Merry Christmas."

"Merry Christmas."

"Hey, merry Christmas, Joe!" Bradley said.

Joe walked over and grabbed Bradley around the waist lifting him upside down, accompanied by his giggles. "Merry Christmas, slick. So you think you've got any presents?"

Between squeals Bradley said, "Sure do. Can I open them now, Mom?"

"Let Joe get a cup of coffee."

Joe set Bradley down and headed for the coffee pot. As he added cream to his coffee, he said quietly, "Dasher's gone." To Mary's questioning eyes he continued, "No trace of him. Just like he was suddenly here, now he's suddenly gone."

"That's because Santa needed him last night. Didn't you know that, Joe?" Bradley asked, clinging to Joe's pants leg.

"I guess I forgot, little monkey," Joe said smiling.

In the parlor, Bradley gasped at all the presents and ran to the tree.

Mary and Joe followed, each carrying a mug of coffee. "Remember, Bradley that not all of those presents are for you."

"Presents!" Jenna squealed as she came into the room followed by Kevin. Celia and Richard were close behind, their eyes half-closed and unfocused.

When Richard saw the mug of coffee in Joe's hand he whimpered. "Where'd you get that?"

"There's a pot in the kitchen," Mary said. "I'll get you—"

"No, I've got it. Want a cup, sweetheart?" Richard asked Celia.

"Yes, please." Her eyes adored her husband.

Joe put his arm around Mary, pleased that Richard had come to his senses.

"What's all this?" Lila said coming into the parlor.

"It's Christmas, Miss Lila!" Bradley exclaimed.

"So, I see. Looks like some kids have been real good," she said.

"Why can't some kids be real good later in the morning?" Dan asked from the door of the parlor.

"Dan, why don't you go back to sleep?" Mary asked.

He walked over and draped his arm around Lila's shoulder. "Because my girl loves Christmas morning so therefore, I love Christmas morning."

"Smart man," Joe said chuckling.

By the time all the adults had their coffee and were seated, Bradley had pretty much separated the gifts into piles. Given the signal from their moms, the kids ripped into the presents.

"My goodness, why didn't someone wake me?" Angela said as she came into the room.

"We thought we'd let you sleep," Mary said.

"And miss these precious little ones and their gifts? Not on your life."

241

"Mom! Look! I got a new sled! Can we try it out today Joe?"

"You bet we can." When Mary's eyes questioned his, Joe whispered, "I picked up the sled before the blizzard. Sam said that Bradley would love it."

"I'm surprised Sam's not here for this," Mary said.

"Um, I'm afraid Sam and Eldon have left." All eyes turned to Angela, waiting for an explanation. "Well you see, they said they needed to leave last night. I said I'd send their goodbyes along to everyone."

"That seems awful sudden. Was everything all right?" Joe asked.

"Yes. They just wanted to get home and since the weather had cleared they decided to go on ahead. Oh, Jenna, what a beautiful doll."

"It's an angel. Just like I was in the play last night! She's beautiful!"

Celia and Richard looked at each other. "I didn't, did you?" Celia asked.

"No. I didn't."

Angela winked at the confused parents. Celia mouthed the words "thank you."

"Hey, what's this?" Kevin asked as he found a small box that said "To the Davis Family."

"Well, why don't you open it up?" Richard said.

Kevin opened the box and read the note inside. As he finished reading, he started hooping and hollering and ran to jump on his dad hugging him tightly. Jenna picked up the note and read.

With a loud squeal, she joined her brother and showered her father with kisses all over his face.

Richard was laughing but caught his breath enough to say, "Maybe you should show the note to your mother." Her face beaming, Jenna handed the note to Celia.

It read: St. Tropez for one cancelled. Disney World for four confirmed.

Celia's hand trembled as she read the note. Tears poured from her eyes, as she truly believed now that they were a family again. Richard reached over and pulled her close to him. Celia rested her head against his chest, breathing deeply, contentedly.

Joe and Mary sat on the floor with Bradley looking at all his gifts. Lila and Dan snuggled together on a couch, sharing quiet conversation. The Davis family still hugged on the other couch, discussing which rides and attractions to go on first.

Angela sighed with happiness.

The telephone ringing in the reception area broke into her reverie as she walked into the hallway to answer, closing the doors of the parlor.

"Merry Christmas," she answered.

"Merry Christmas, Angela. Just wanted to call and see how everything is this morning?" Sam's deep voice filled with laughter warmed her spirit.

"Everything is better that great. So you and the elf made it back safely? Dasher too?"

"Even with all his complaining, yes. Eldon, that is, not Dasher."

"I forgot to tell you. The reindeer was a nice touch. Very nice."

"Thanks."

"And everything went well for your father last night, I assume?"

"Better that great, as well."

"Excellent. Please give my regards to your family. And thank them profusely for allowing you and Eldon and Dasher to help me out this time. Your rewards will be great, I can promise you. The owner of the inn was very pleased."

"Good to hear. And it really has been our pleasure. It's always an honor to work with you."

"You too . . . 'Sam.'"

"So, tell me. What's going to happen with the good folks at the Sleep in Heavenly Peace Inn?"

"Well, I really shouldn't."

"Come on. Consider it a down payment on that great reward you talk about."

"All right." Angela smiled, happy to share good news. "Mary and Joe will marry soon and have a long and happy marriage, raising Bradley and running the inn."

"Excellent. And the others? What about Lila and Dan?"

"After they visit Dan's friend in Florida, they'll start dating in New York. They'll find out that the other is just what they need to complete their life."

"I'm glad. I sincerely liked them both. What about the Davis family?"

"Celia and Richard are back together to stay, and since talking everything out, they are stronger than ever. In addition, they're taking home more than a few extra gifts from their stay at the inn."

"You don't mean—"

"That's right. Twins. To be born at the beginning of September. Richard will be over the moon. And Jenna and Kevin will dote on their new brother and sister. Celia will treasure her family, remembering the power of simple kindness."

"That's wonderful. A happy family again.

"Aren't you going to ask me about the other two?"

"Who? You mean Genevieve and Bo?"

"They marry, settle down in Montpelier, and raise six children." Angela couldn't help adding, "And Genevieve never gets her figure back."

"Ho, ho, ho! I truly didn't see that coming. Will miracles never cease?"

Angela laughed. "Not as long as I'm here."

Sam's laughter continuing, he said, "Angela. You are an angel."

She smiled, breathing a sigh of satisfaction and said, "That's what they tell me."

THE END

Thank you for reading
Sleep In Heavenly Peace Inn.
I hope you'll take a moment
to leave a review so that
others can find this book.

Thanks so much!!

If you loved *Sleep in Heavenly Peace Inn*, check out the sequel, *Sleep in Heavenly Peace Inn Two*. Turn the page for an excerpt.

Excerpt from
Sleep In Heavenly Peace Two

Mary Michaels felt an itch between her shoulder blades and not one that meant she needed a backscratcher. Something was coming, something that would change lives. But if there was anything that the Sleep In Heavenly Peace Inn excelled in, it was in changing lives.

She'd long ago decided to stop questioning the magic of the inn, knowing that Angela, the manager, would continue to mysteriously know things, the owner would continue to remain benevolent and secretive, and she, her husband Joe, and son Bradley would continue to live and work there with a great deal of happiness.

Pausing from her chore of dusting and glancing out the window, she took a moment to appreciate the beautiful countryside of Vermont, covered with a blanket of snow, the bright blue sky a deep contrast. The weather had been perfect for business this year and reports were that it would continue. Unlike the terrible blizzard they'd had two years ago. Much had changed in that time, and she couldn't be happier. Mary had everything she could ever want. She sighed.

A quick survey of the cozy parlor showed her all was in order, with plump couches and chairs, tables with puzzles at the ready, shelves full of interesting books, and a large hearth already cracking with a comforting fire, ready for the arrival of their guests, as was she. Just as soon as she finished dusting the small table next to the window.

"Mom? Where do you want me to put my shoe?"

It was an unusual question, even from her seven-year old son, who knew better than to be yelling in the inn. "Bradley, you know you aren't suppose to yell inside," she yelled.

Mary was glad Angela was out in the barn and Joe was on his way back from the airport to miss her hypocrisy.

The young boy appeared in the doorway clothed in his heavy coat, woolen hat, his cheeks pink from the cold weather. Holding a sneaker dripping in mud.

She gasped. "Bradley! You're making a mess all over the foyer!" She dropped her duster and ran to take the shoe from him, her eyes following the trail that disappeared down the hall to the kitchen door.

"It wasn't my fault. The mud puddle just came out of nowhere."

"Why didn't you have on your boots?" She handed the shoe back to him and took off her apron to use as a mop. As she cleaned, Bradley followed, carrying the offending shoe and unbeknownst to her, making another muddy trail.

"I forgot. I was in the kitchen getting a drink of water and when I looked out the window, I saw the best dog in the world! He was big and hairy and he was smiling at me. Then he turned around and started running away. I couldn't let him get away before I met him." He paused and as if thinking to impress his mother with his manners, said, "That would be rude."

Mary snorted. "So you didn't take the time to put your boots on, got it."

"Yeah, he ran to the mud by the hot pool."

"Tub."

"Yeah, tub. So, where do you want me to put this shoe?"

"How about outside so we can hose it down. By the way, what happened to the—"

She opened the door to the kitchen and froze at the sight. A furry monster was currently making himself comfortable on her clean, polished floor, his body squirming and shaking, flinging mud everywhere. Mary heard a scream and a second later realized it was her.

The dog looked up, gave Bradley a doggy smile and then bolted over, his big body knocking the boy down on his bottom. After a loud bark, the dog pushed through the door and down the hall.

"Noooo!" Mary gathered her wits and tore off after the dog. He'd made it to the front parlor before she found him, making himself at home on one of the couches. She calmed her voice and said, "All right, dog. It's time you came with me. Okay? I have a treat for you in the kitchen. Don't you want a delicious treat?"

The dog cocked his head with an expression that seemed to show his amusement. She could almost hear him thinking, "You think I'm that stupid?" Mary walked carefully toward the couch, getting ready to grab the dog. There was no collar, nothing she could grab. Which meant she was going to have to wrap her arms around the dog and drag him out.

After another couple of steps, she quickly jumped onto the couch, just as the dog moved away, barking at the new game. Bradley joined into the fray, trying to corral the happy dog. Neither could grab hold and the dog slipped back into the foyer, lying on his back on the wood floor, emitting a contented moan as he wiggled back and forth. When Mary and Bradley caught up with him, the game began again. She was so engrossed in chasing the dog, she didn't notice the front door opening.

She made a desperate last lunge and captured the dog against her body. "Aha, now I've got you." Sensing they weren't alone, she glanced at the door.

Their guests had arrived.

Two of the four guests appeared bewildered. The other two, a handsome couple, arm-in-arm, grinned. Mary let out a frustrated breath.

Before she could say anything, the back door opened and Angela came in, her eyes coming to rest on the dog. Mary watched in awe as the dog settled in her grasp, his tongue hanging from his mouth, panting, staring at the inn's manager.

"Well, what do we have here?"

"I am so sorry, Angela. I'm afraid we had an unexpected guest drop in. We'll get the dog outside and the inn back in order immediately."

Her face heated as she faced her guests and said, "Ah, welcome, everyone."

She stood just as her husband Joe, the inn's handyman, came in carrying luggage. When he grinned at the sight of the dog, Bradley, her, and a mud-splattered foyer, she wanted to slug him. His eyes went to the panting dog. "I don't believe I've met our new decorator." The one couple chuckled. Mary hoped they all didn't just turn around and head out the door.

She pushed back her dark hair, now sporting a speck or two of mud and walked forward. "I'm so sorry for the mess, folks." She glared at the dog, who seemed to smile at her. "Please come in and Angela will get you settled."

"Joe, perhaps you can take the dog outside," Angela said, not moving an inch. Joe immediately walked to the dog, picking him up and heading out the back door. Angela clapped her hands together, as if the last few minutes had not been chaos or the inn was not a mess of mud and dog slobber. "We are so glad to have you folks for the Christmas holidays. Please come over to the desk and I'll give you your keys.

"I am so sorry," Mary whispered as she walked past the woman to begin the cleanup.

In the kitchen, she found a remorseful Bradley waiting for her. "I put the shoe outside. Like you told me to."

She wanted to stay mad, wanted to scold and punish and lecture. But his big eyes, so like the father he had lost years ago, melted all anger away. With a slight grin, she said, "It *was* a cool dog."

Walking to the mudroom, she pulled out all the cleaning supplies she'd need to set things to right.

Bradley followed. "Wasn't he? Can I keep him? Can I keep Fred?"

"Oh, hold on a minute. I think first—wait, Fred?"

"Yep. That's what I'm going to name him. Fred after Mr. Fred, the crossing guard at school."

Her interest peaked, she turned to him. "Ah, that's so nice. Very thoughtful that you'd name a pet after someone you admire."

"Huh? Nah, it's because Mr. Fred looks like a dog." Mary shook her head. "He has those droopy eyes and that big mustache and his hair—"

"Yes, I get it. But like I was saying, first we have to find out if the dog belongs to someone and return him. Even if he doesn't, we've already got one dog, one horse, three sheep, one cow, two chickens, and a duck out in the barn. I think that's plenty of animals, don't you?"

"But old rover is lonely for another dog. This one could be a playmate for him, don't you think?"

Her hands filled with rags and cleaners, she walked back to the kitchen. "Son, you know that the inn doesn't belong to us. We have to follow the owner's rules. He only takes in abused and homeless animals. Someone may be looking for this dog."

"But if they aren't?"

She sighed. "I'll see what Angela says." Bradley whooped and ran to the mudroom. "Hold on, just a minute." Her words had him sliding to a halt. "You helped make this mess by bringing that dog in so you're going to help clean it up." She threw a rag to him and said, "Let's get started."

Angela smiled warmly and then sat behind her desk, ready to receive the guests.

A tall statuesque couple approached. Angela already liked them for their amusement over the dog. "I'm Darren Matthews and this is my wife Tricia. I believe we have a suite?" he said with a slight southern drawl.

The couple was striking, each tall, with brown hair, although his was a lighter shade while hers was a deep mahogany. The man smiled easily as he looked around whereas the wife wrapped her arm around his, waiting for their key.

"Of course, Mr. Matthews. You and your wife have the 'It's a Wonderful Life Suite.' Here's your key. It's the last door on the right on the second floor. Joe will be right up with your luggage."

"Thank you." The couple started for the stairs and the wife turned to ask, "When is dinner?"

"Dinner is served each night at six-thirty."

The woman, Tricia, gave her husband a knowing smile. "Perfect. Come on, darlin.'" Darren gave a nod and followed his wife upstairs.

Angela watched them go, wondering when she'd seen a happier couple. Well, that was about to change. She'd have to be vigilant, compassionate, see that they both got the understanding they needed.

"Excuse, but we are waiting."

She turned back to the beautiful and irritated woman with the foreign accent standing before her. Her hair, which was styled in an elegant chignon at the back of her neck, was dark as midnight, her eyes wide and golden. Her face was beautiful, the makeup applied perfectly. Unfortunately, she was not smiling.

"I'm sorry. You are—"

"Natasha Safina. My manager made the reservations. I am performing in Stowe, Vermont."

"Yes, dear, I know."

The man behind her quickly inserted himself. "And I am Franklin Murray, pianist extraordinaire. Perhaps you have heard of me." The man's intonation was precise, very proper British.

"Well, of course I've heard of you and Miss Safina. That's why we booked you two."

The twosome glanced at each other and then at Angela. "You mean we are performing . . . here? At little inn?" Natasha began muttering in Russian, explaining why she didn't think it was a good idea and her plans for her manager once she got a hold of him. Angela wondered if she should tell the woman that she spoke fluent Russian.

"I'm sorry, but I am a little confused. You mean our manager booked us to perform here?" Franklin looked around. "At the Sleep In Heavenly Peace Inn? I don't understand."

"We decided to spice things up this year and have live entertainment. Now, we'll expect you nightly in the parlor—Mr. Murray, we have a small spinet there and Miss Safina . . . well, you have your own violin. Then from ten to eleven, in our small lounge. There we have a keyboard. We have a lovely music room down the hall with another piano. It's very quiet there. You two are welcome to practice there anytime you wish." She handed a key to each of them. "Miss Safina, you have 'The Grinch that Stole Christmas' room and Mr. Murray, the 'White Christmas' room. Second floor. Joe will have your bags up soon.

The woman became incensed. "I do not have suite? I must have suite to meditate. To practice. I cannot be my best if I have to live in little room."

"We only have one suite and it's been booked for months. But I'm sure you'll enjoy our Grinch room. It is quite charming."

"And what is Grinch?" Franklin was chuckling under his breath.

"It's a famous book from Dr. Seuss about a . . . well, there's a copy in your room. When you get the chance perhaps you'd like to read it. It really is a wonderful story."

"I do not want to read medical book by this doctor." Again, she began muttering in Russian about the ridiculousness of the situation and the ancestry of her despised manager. She turned away pulling out her phone, clearly to get said manager on the line.

Franklin watched her, shaking his head, then turned to Angela. "I'm sure the rooms will be satisfactory, Ms. . . . ."

"Just call me Angela, Mr. Murray." Ignoring Natasha's rants, she added, "We are all very much looking forward to hearing you two perform. I'll see you at dinner tonight."

"Yes, thank you." Franklin walked to the stairs, also ignoring Natasha, who followed him, her rantings echoing through the inn.

She breathed deeply and looked heavenward, praying for strength. Glancing down at the reservation book, she smiled. They weren't finished receiving guests yet.

It was shaping up to be an interesting Christmas.

Sleep In Heavenly Peace Inn Two
Available now at online bookstores.

Your free books are waiting!

Do you enjoy sweet romance, holiday stories, Christian Fiction?

You can get three stories for free. That's right, three! It's a special gift to you for signing up for Malinda Martin's monthly newsletter.

To get your free books, go to www.malindamartin.com. You'll also receive information on other sweet romance and Christian fiction novels.

Dear Friend,

Thank you so much for reading Sleep in Heavenly Peace Inn. This was one of the first romance stories I wrote and it continues to be a favorite. I've always believed in miracles, especially at Christmas, and it was fun to bring a few to life in this book.

People ask me how I created this story. Years ago, before Biff and I had children, we visited Stowe, Vermont one year after Christmas, staying at a charming bed and breakfast inn. On the way to the ski resort, there was a large farmhouse off the main road, set against the backdrop of the mountains. Beautiful. It was the perfect setting for a Christmas story. And the name, other than, of course, coming from the song, came from a visit to one of my favorite hotels, The Inn at Christmas Place in Pigeon Forge, Tennessee. The company that supplies their mattresses and pillows is called The Sleep in Heavenly Peace Company. I loved it! Perfect. So, what else could I use that name for? Hmm. How about an inn?

The story still brings hope to me and I pray to you as well. May we always see the goodness, the kindness, the love that originated at the first Christmas thousands of years ago. Merry Christmas!

Blessings,
M.M.

Made in United States
North Haven, CT
24 November 2022